THE RISSOLE MYSTERY

Borgo Press Books by S. Fowler Wright

Arresting Delia: An Inspector Cleveland Classic Crime Novel
The Attic Murder: An Inspector Combridge & Mr. Jellipot Classic Crime Novel
The Bell Street Murders: An Inspector Combridge & Mr. Jellipot Classic Crime Novel
Beyond the Rim: A Lost Race Fantasy
Black Widow: A Classic Crime Novel
The Capone Caper: Mr. Jellipot vs. the King of Crime: A Classic Crime Novel
Crime & Co.: An Inspector Cleveland Classic Crime Novel
Dawn: A Novel of Global Warming
Dead by Saturday: An Inspector Cleveland Classic Crime Novel
Dream; or, The Simian Maid: A Fantasy of Prehistory (Marguerite Cranleigh #1)
Elfwin: An Historical Novel of Anglo-Saxon Times
The End of the Mildew Gang: An Inspector Cauldron Classic Crime Novel (Mildew Gang #3)
Four Callers in Razor Street: An Inspector Combridge & Mr. Jellipot Classic Crime Novel
The Hanging of Constance Hillier: An Inspector Cleveland Classic Crime Novel
The Hidden Tribe: A Lost Race Fantasy
The Jordans Murder: An Inspector Combridge & Mr. Jellipot Classic Crime Novel
The King Against Anne Bickerton: A Classic Crime Novel
The Mildew Gang: An Inspector Cauldron Classic Crime Novel (Mildew Gang #1)
Murder in Bethnal Square: An Inspector Combridge & Mr. Jellipot Classic Crime Novel
The Police and the Public: Some Thoughts on the British System of Justice
Post-Mortem Evidence: An Inspector Combridge & Mr. Jellipot Classic Crime Novel
The Return of the Mildew Gang: An Inspector Cauldron Classic Crime Novel (Mildew Gang #2)
The Rissole Mystery: An Inspector Combridge & Mr. Jellipot Classic Crime Novel
The Screaming Lake: A Lost Race Fantasy
The Secret of the Screen: An Inspector Combridge & Mr. Jellipot Classic Crime Novel
Spiders' War: A Novel of the Far Future (Marguerite Cranleigh #3)
Three Witnesses: A Classic Crime Novel
Too Much for Mr. Jellipot: An Inspector Combridge & Mr. Jellipot Classic Crime Novel
The Vengeance of Gwa: A Fantasy of Prehistory (Marguerite Cranleigh #2)
Was Murder Done? A Classic Crime Novel
Who Murdered Reynard? A Classic Crime Novel
The Wills of Jane Kanwhistle: An Inspector Combridge & Mr. Jellipot Classic Crime Novel
With Cause Enough?: An Inspector Combridge & Mr. Jellipot Classic Crime Novel

THE RISSOLE MYSTERY

AN INSPECTOR COMBRIDGE AND MR. JELLIPOT CLASSIC CRIME NOVEL

by

S. FOWLER WRIGHT

WRITING AS "SYDNEY FOWLER"

THE BORGO PRESS

An Imprint of Wildside Press LLC

MMIX

CONTENTS

Chapter I: A Letter for Scotland Yard 7
Chapter II: The Anxiety of Jane Lovejoy 10
Chapter III: Mr. Rissole 13
Chapter IV: Concerning Motive and Opportunity 17
Chapter V: Mr. Lovejoy Has a Good Appetite 22
Chapter VI: Fingerprints from the Lovejoys................................ 27
Chapter VII: Why Mr. Lovejoy Was Short of Cash 30
Chapter VIII: Some Information from Mr. Jellipot 34
Chapter IX: Mr. Jellipot Consults His Clerk 38
Chapter X: A Surprising Action by Mr. Jellipot.......................... 42
Chapter XI: The Banker Is Pleased to Lend 50
Chapter XII: The Tenants on the Ground Floor............................ 55
Chapter XIII: A Quarrel at Lovejoy's Flat................................... 60
Chapter XIV: The Misses Ranger Were Shocked 67
Chapter XV: The Opinion of Mr. Jellipot.................................... 72
Chapter XVI: The Trailing of Tony Rissole 79
Chapter XVII: A Procedure in Reverse 85
Chapter XVIII: The First Interview of the Day Before 89
Chapter XIX: The Second Interview of the Day Before............... 93
Chapter XX: Mr. Jellipot Makes His Choice.............................. 101
Chapter XXI: What Vestman Had to Tell.................................... 104
Chapter XXII: Tony Is for the Dock... 111
Chapter XXIII: Mr. Jellipot Finds That Admiration Can Go
    Too Far.. 115
Chapter XXIV: Mr. Jellipot Has Time for Thought 121
Chapter XXV: Mr. Jellipot Breaks a Cup 126
Chapter XXVI: The Consequences of Breaking China 133
Chapter XXVII: A Damning Fact... 136
Chapter XXVIII: Mr. Jellipot Gives His Reasons 140
Chapter XXIX: "It Isn't Possible" 145
Chapter XXX: A Quandary for the Yard 149
Chapter XXXI: Mr. Jellipot Does a Good Deed......................... 154

Chapter XXXII: It Was as Simple as That.................................... 160

CHAPTER I.

A LETTER FOR SCOTLAND YARD

IT was Monday morning, only a few days after the Jordans murder case had collapsed in a manner so disconcerting to the official mind,[1] and Chief Inspector Combridge was in no very confident mood, when he entered Superintendent Davis's office, and that gentleman passed a letter across his desk, with the remark: "If you've got nothing better to do this morning, it might be worthwhile to look into this."

Chief Inspector Combridge took the letter without eagerness, and read it without enthusiasm. Had it come from any other, hand, and had not his reputation been too securely established to be shaken by a single failure, he would have suspected that he was being deliberately put upon a trivial investigation, as a sign of official displeasure.

The letter was brief, and of a class of communication, usually though not always anonymous, which is continually being received at the headquarters of the investigation of metropolitan crime. Someone has seen a figure lurk in the dusk, or move behind the blind of what should have been an empty house—a quarrelsome wife is said to have left home suddenly, and the neighbours surmise that it is to an address from which there is no return—a door from which a figure would emerge regularly at a morning hour has remained closed—a whisper was overheard indicating a plotted crime.

Such communications are always investigated, although the vast majority of them are the products of idle imagination, or misdirected spite. Such enquiries require discretion as well as acumen. They are excellent training for the younger members of the force, but rarely engage the attention of its superior officers.

Now Inspector Combridge read:

---

[1] See *The Jordans Murder*.

4 Barclay Buildings, Lower Sloane Street, S.W.1.
February 28, 193—

The Commissioner of Police,
New Scotland Yard, London

Dear Sir,

The flat on the floor below the above address is occupied by Mr. Adrian Rissole, a retired ship steward, who lives alone.

For the last week, more or less, he has not been observed to enter or leave, and does not answer the door.

Both my wife and myself are rather anxious as to what the explanation may be, as we think it unlikely that Mr. Rissole would have gone away, and it seems best to advise you of the position.

Yours faithfully,

Edwin Lovejoy

"You think," the inspector said, when he had read this letter twice over, with his customary care, "that there may be something here?"

Superintendent Davis, as is the case with many heavily-built, slow-moving men, was not wasteful of words. He replied: "Well, what do you think?"

"I couldn't make more than a poor guess. It's the letter of a fairly educated man. Rather stiff, as though he'd composed it carefully. He's particular to mention his wife, and it's ten to one that, if she hadn't badgered him into doing it, he'd never have written at all. I should say that there's nothing in it, about fifty times more likely than not. There's no reason why a retired ship steward shouldn't take a week's holiday without first informing the lady on the floor above.

"On the other hand, a man living alone is always liable to be attacked, especially if he's supposed to have any money hidden away, as those who have given up work often have.

"But it's just as likely—I should say a lot more so—that he's fallen ill and been unable to call for help. That is, if there's anything in it at all."

"Looked at that way," the superintendent suggested, "it seems a bit callous to waste time sending a letter through the weekend post."

"Yes. It would have been a lot quicker to ring us up. But if the man didn't think there was any occasion to write at all——"

"Well, you might just clear it up. It may be one of those cases where the lady has used her eyes in the right way."

Chief Inspector Combridge got up to go. He turned the letter over, as though looking for those elusive clues which are the favourite theme of the writers of detective fiction. Perhaps he was; but, if so, he caught no more than one of the worthless fish which a good angler will throw back contemptuously to the water from which they come.

"Woolworth paper," he said. "There's not much to be learnt from that." There would not have been much even had he been dealing with an anonymous communication, for such paper is purchased by people of widely differing social grades.

Beyond that, his experienced mind had already formed a vague but yet accurate impression of the type of man from whom such a letter must have come.

"Fairly educated," he had said in his first reaction to what he read. He did not analyse the basis of this conclusion. He had not had a classical education himself. But he knew subconsciously that a good linguist, in a letter as deliberately written as that one evidently was, would not use the ugly colloquialism "answer the door."

"I think I'll have a few words with Mr. Lovejoy," he remarked, as he went out; but that was not to be his initial experience in an investigation which would fully occupy him during the next fortnight; for, when he pressed the bell at 4 Barclay Buildings, it was Mrs. Lovejoy who opened the door, and asked him in to an otherwise empty flat.

CHAPTER II.

The Anxiety of Jane Lovejoy

CHIEF INSPECTOR COMBRIDGE looked at a pretty and attractive young woman. So youthful, indeed, that he would have called her "Miss" without hesitation, apart from the witness of her own lips, and the wedding ring that she wore.

She received him without embarrassment. Her expression, as he showed his card, actually seemed to be one of relief, as though she would not have been surprised to have to face a less welcome visitor. It was not a reception of which he could reasonably complain, but it was sufficiently unusual to be noticed by one more familiar with experiences of an opposite kind. There are timid women, even of the most blameless lives, who will become visibly perturbed on opening their door to find that a policeman is on the mat.

Still, after the letter which her husband had written, more or less at her own instigation, she must have been prepared for his appearance. He recognized that; and yet subtly her attitude increased the anticipation that he was not wasting time which should have been more profitably employed.

"You'd better come in," she said, "and I'll explain why my husband wrote."

She led the way to a rather drab room, obviously furnished from a hire-purchase stock, but with some evidences that it was occupied by those who made the best of their narrow means.

"I'm glad you've come," she went on, as she stooped to put a match to the gas fire. "I've been really worried as to what can have happened; though I ought to tell you that Mr. Lovejoy thinks I'm making a fuss about nothing. He didn't want to write to you, only I couldn't rest unless something were done."

"You know Mr. Rissole?"

"Yes. We have been very friendly. That's what makes me feel sure he wouldn't have gone away without letting us know."

"Nothing more than that?"

"Well, it seems to me it's a good deal. We've known him for more than a year—ever since we came here—and he's been coming up in the evening for a game of draughts or backgammon with Mr. Lovejoy about twice a week; and sometimes we go down to him. I don't think that he's ever been away for a night during the whole time, or ever spoken of going anywhere. He's led a quiet regular life.

"You see, he's not very young—I don't mean he's really old—and he's rather lame. There was an accident on his ship. A capstan or something fell on his leg. It wasn't what I could understand. But I know he got some compensation, and retired earlier than he would have done in the ordinary way."

"You mean he's a lame man, who can't get about properly?"

"Oh no! He's not a cripple. I didn't mean you to think that. But he walks a bit lame. He goes for a walk every morning—I mean he did. And he goes to football matches, and things like that. I think the football pools were the greatest interest that he had."

Inspector Combridge noticed the unconscious use of the past tense in that final phrase. Did she know more than he had yet been told? Had she more cause to suspect? But her manner was quiet and frank. Perhaps it was natural enough! He knew that those who adopt a mood of suspicion are too apt to find what they seek to see. He asked: "When did you see him last?"

"It was Thursday. Not last Thursday—the one before. So, counting today, it's more than ten days ago. He was up here just as usual then, and I feel sure he would have mentioned it if he had been meaning to go away."

"That sounds likely enough. But he might not have known he was going when he was here. He might have decided later, or had some sudden call, such as a relative's illness. I can't say that there's anything conclusive in that."

"Perhaps not. But you can see what risks there are for anyone living alone. I think something ought to be done to make sure."

"Yes. I see how you feel. But, from our point of view, it's very difficult to do anything. We can't break into people's flats just because they take a week's holiday. We've no legal right, and we should become unpopular if we tried it on."

"Then you will just leave it, and do nothing?"

There was a note of anxiety in her voice which again seemed to the inspector to be rather more than the occasion required, and to indicate a sharper concern than neighbourly regard would be likely to rouse. He reminded himself that women are apt to be emotional with what may seem inadequate cause to the masculine mind, and was cynical enough to wonder whether a mere morbid curiosity, as an alternative explanation; might not be disguising itself in a better dress. But she seemed simple, sincere, and genuinely forgetful of herself in consideration of her neighbour's possible need. He said: "You seem to be worrying about this a good deal. You must have known Mr. Rissole rather intimately?"

"Yes. I told you that. We were, as far as I know, the only friends that he had."

This reply came without embarrassment, and as freely as before. It reduced another possibility which had come to a mind familiar with so many aspects of human weakness. Was it not possible that Mrs. Lovejoy might have been on even closer terms of intimacy with the occupant of the flat below than her husband suspected? Did she know of some reason for attributing a sinister explanation to his absence, such as she could not disclose without admitting more than she could afford to do? In her husband's absence, which might be for long regular hours during the day, how solitary, how free from observation, these two people would have been—the young recently married girl on the top floor of the house, and the retired steward who was "not old," alone in the flat below! Who could say that they had only met in the evening hours? He knew the danger of speculating in advance of the facts he had. But what actresses some women are! His mind in more doubts than one, he answered merely: "Well, I'll have a look at the flat."

He did not expect to learn much from inspecting a closed door. He wanted time to decide what he should do next.

CHAPTER III.

MR. RISSOLE

BARCLAY BUILDINGS do not consist of flats of a modern type. It is a case of a row of old houses of outward respectability being converted into a series of separate flats, one on each floor, by the provision of bathrooms and a minimum of kitchen accommodation. There are no lifts. There is a single porter whose duties pertain to the whole row. The door before which the inspector paused had not even the security of a modern lock. It was one which would be very easy to pick. He reflected that it was a door which anyone having a hostile purpose would quickly enter. An elderly or crippled man, living alone in such a place, and perhaps watched when drawing money and taking it home, almost asked for trouble.

But he saw something else. There was a pint milk bottle on a window ledge by the door.

He prised up the cardboard stopper, and saw that the milk was fresh. If milk were being taken in daily, he had been brought there by one of the emptiest tales that had ever wasted the time of the Yard. "We'll see," he thought, "what the young woman has to say to this." He went back upstairs.

Mrs; Lovejoy heard him without surprise. "Oh yes," she said. "I ought to have told you that. The milkman spoke to me about it. He said he'd had no orders to stop supplies, so he had been putting a fresh bottle there at every round, and taking the old one away. "

He considered this, and saw that it rather increased the probability that something was wrong. If Mr. Rissole had gone away, he had not only failed to notify his neighbours on the floor above (which he had been under no obligation to do), he had also omitted to inform one at least of the tradesmen with whom he dealt. He went down again to the closed door. He pressed for a long second upon the bell.

He knew that one very competent member of the force would argue seriously that a bell has a different sound in a deserted house, and that it is possible to tell thereby, after ringing once, when persistence will be rewarded and when it will be a saving of time to withdraw. That may be true or not, but now, aided by imagination or fact, he felt that the bell sounded a note of desertion. He would have been almost startled had he heard an approaching step, or seen the door open to confront him with a living man.

He pushed open a letter flap which had no box on its inner side, and saw a thin scatter of letters or circulars on the floor.

He looked with some attention at the lock, which he was now disposed to pick. He observed that it had no key on the inner side. He saw that to be a singular fact if it had been locked (and locked it certainly was) on the inside, but natural if someone had gone away after securing it from without, in which event he would have taken the key with him. It was equally natural whether Mr. Rissole himself had taken it, as his right was, or it had been used in the same way by a fleeing criminal, who would not be likely to simplify discovery by leaving an open door behind him.

In fact, the absence of the key showed no more than that the flat was most probably empty.

Yet that was something. It decreased the likelihood that, if he should force the door, he would come upon a man quietly eating his lunch, or perhaps sleeping off the effects of some weekend indulgence, who would ask unpleasant questions as to his justification for trespassing there.

It was the kind of dilemma which his department had to face continually, and in which no excuse, however good, was of much avail, either for mistaken action or for inaction at the wrong time. What his superiors expected was that he should make the right guess, and it is by the instinctive capacity for such decisions that officers in the detective service avoid censure, and rise to such conspicuous positions as that which Chief Inspector Combridge already held.

He considered that there should be a porter in charge of such buildings, one who would probably have a master key, and who might enter the flat with a better right than himself, though perhaps not much.

He might have asked Mrs. Lovejoy that. In two minutes he might do so still. But he was indisposed to make further enquiries from her. There were two flats below. He would hear what their occupants had to say.

That proved to be simpler to resolve than to do. The first floor flat was untenanted. That on the ground floor appeared to be occupied, but efforts with bell and knocker produced no reply.

Used to meeting such obstacles, and to overcoming them by patient pertinacity, he went on to the next house.

Here the first door at which he rang supplied him with the address of the porter, who lived on the other side of the road. He learned also that the man would be unlikely to be at home at that hour. But his wife might.

So it proved. Mrs. Neasom, a gaunt woman with a baby on her arm, said that her husband would be out till one o'clock. She knew Mr. Rissole. He lived at number three. She could not say that she had seen him for some days, but she evidently saw nothing singular in that circumstance. She described him as a quiet, pleasant gentleman. Elderly? Well, you might say. And lame? Yes, a little. Not much to notice. Not when you got used to it. She hoped there was nothing wrong?

Inspector Combridge saw that her idea of anything being wrong was of some trouble coming from the police, rather than of illness or misadventure which they should relieve. To avert that familiar form of misunderstanding, he gave a brief explanation of the enquiry which he was making.

Mrs. Neasom appeared unimpressed. She thought Mr. Rissole to be quite capable of looking after himself. She said darkly that she should have thought the Lovejoys had got enough to do minding their own affairs.

As to a key for the flat, she had none to offer, even had she shown more disposition to help. Nor would her husband be able to do more if he were in. Their duties were with the main doors and lights, and to keep stairs and passages clean.

Inspector Combridge saw that she took a common-sense view of the matter, with which he was still half inclined to agree. But he did not fail to observe that the isolation of those two upstairs flats was more absolute, both by day and night, than he had previously supposed.

He turned the conversation to the Lovejoys. He learned that Edwin Lovejoy was an ironmonger. He had a business in the Hornsey Road. The woman evidently knew something more about these tenants which she was reluctant to say. He did not press for what might have been no more than irrelevant gossip. The whole enquiry seemed too likely to end in nothing. If he should want more information, he was content to know that it could be had here. But he had decided to resolve the matter by entering the almost certainly empty flat.

The keyless lock would be easy to open in such a manner that there would be no remaining evidence of his lawless action. In all probability, if no irregularity had occurred to justify his invasion, it would be an interference which might remain unguessed. He could advise the Lovejoys to maintain silence, which they should be very willing to promise. At the worst, there was the husband's letter to give occasion for what he did. He sought an ironmonger, avoiding the Hornsey Road, procured the keys that such a lock would require, and entered the flat without difficulty.

As he entered the little ill-kept sitting-room, he knew that he would not be called to account for that illegally opened door. The foul odour which met him had already prepared his eyes for the sight upon which they fell.

That which had been Adrian Rissole ten days before lay face downwards upon the floor.

CHAPTER IV.

CONCERNING MOTIVE AND OPPORTUNITY

THE dead man lay with his feet towards the door, his face in the wool hearthrug. There was no sign of a struggle. No disorder in a room which was over-furnished in a shabby way, and in the style of an earlier period. A room the walls and mantelpiece of which were covered with dusty portraits and knickknacks, as was the top of the ancient roll-top desk, and where any violence of movement would have produced a chaos not easily to have been straightened again.

He had been stabbed in the back. It was a wound which could not have been self-inflicted. It had been deep and wide, and had bled as such wounds will not always do. The inspector judged that Adrian Rissole had fallen as he was struck.

He might well have been dead for a week, but that was for the medical gentlemen to decide.

He concluded this without touching the body. It was not a case where anything need be hastily done. Not one where the murderer was to be captured by swift pursuit.

He withdrew from the flat, locking the door again, and after a moment's hesitation as to whether he should acquaint Mrs. Lovejoy with his discovery, and request the use of her telephone, went downstairs instead of up, and entered a street call-box. It might be discourteous treatment of those who had led him to the discovery of the crime, but there are circumstances under which courtesy cannot be a paramount consideration to the officers of the C.I.D.

Having acquainted Superintendent Davis with the discovery which he had made, and summoned the expert assistance which such an investigation requires, he went back to Barclay Buildings. He still did not feel it necessary or desirable to ascend to the fourth floor. The time when it would be necessary to interview Mr. Edwin Lovejoy could not be far ahead, but he wished to learn first what he could from inspection of the dead man's flat.

17

The result of this detailed inspection, and of information which came to him during the afternoon, confirmed the discretion of the attitude which he had adopted. When he knocked again at the Lovejoys' door at 6:45 P.M., it was with the knowledge that Edwin Lovejoy had ascended the stairs a few minutes before, and after he had ascertained such facts as, while they fell far short of implicating the tenants of the upper floor in the crime, yet led to a grave doubt concerning the innocence of the man he was about to interview, and of the motives prompting the letter which had originated the investigation.

Had Mr. Lovejoy, he wondered, written reluctantly under the pressure of his wife's urgent importunity? Or had he, perhaps, coldly calculated that it was an action likely to divert suspicion from himself? Was it not possible that Edwin Lovejoy was the one man in the world—perhaps the only one—who knew of the corpse which lay rotting in the sordid disorderly room that would be directly below his feet as he indulged in the comfort of his evening meal? Was it too wild a guess that he had spent the last days in nervous calculation as to when and how the murder would be discovered, as it surely must be at last, and now, with his plans fully formed, his answers to every possible question prepared, had decided that a little friendly concern as to the welfare of their next-floor neighbour would be natural for him and his wife to show? Well, Inspector Combridge concluded, he would be able to judge better when he had seen the man.

He might know more—much more—when certain fingerprints had been developed, and when he had ascertained how Mr. Lovejoy had spent the latter part of the Saturday and the Sunday a week before.

The facts with which he had become armed for his interview with Mr. Lovejoy were briefly these: Adrian Rissole had been stabbed in the back with a broad-bladed weapon such as a carving-knife. The position of the wound indicated that the attack had been furtive and unexpected, and this was supported by the absence of any sign of a struggle in the untidy room. The exact nature of the weapon used must be a matter of conjecture, though it could scarcely be one which most men would have in their possession when paying a friendly call. But it might be one such as an iron-monger could easily select from his own stock, without the risk of a purchase which might be brought in evidence against him.

The opportunity for striking such a blow at Adrian Rissole's back would be more likely to be offered to an acquaintance than a stranger. Men do not commonly admit those whom they do not know into their living rooms and then turn their backs upon them. It is possible to postulate a variety of circumstances under which this might happen, yet it remains a fact that normally it would not. But Edwin Lovejoy was an acquaintance, or, on his own wife's testimony, something more. On her word also, Mr. Rissole's other friends were few, or perhaps, none.

Suppose that Mr. Lovejoy had brought cutlery for his neighbour to consider purchasing? How easy the crime would have been! The lonely flat, without even a resident caretaker to consider—the sudden blow, too unexpected for any outcry before, too savagely deep for more than a choking groan after it had been driven in. Yes, there had been no absence of opportunity.

And motive? Yes, if the Lovejoys knew or suspected the nature of the dead man's will, even apart from any money which they might have known—might be the only outsiders who knew—the flat to contain. For everything that he had, including a capital sum which brought in about three pounds ten a week, was left to Adrian Rissole's "kind friend Jane Lovejoy, who had done so much to cheer the days of a lonely man." That was the wording of the will which had lain in the old-fashioned roll-top desk, which had no better lock than a common penknife could force open, leaving no more evidence than a scratch when it should be closed again—and several scratches were there.

There was here a clear motive of greed; or—perhaps rather less probably—jealousy might have urged the blow. Suppose that Edwin Lovejoy, whether or not he might be aware of the will, had observed a degree of intimacy between the dead man and his wife which he had not liked, and had thus been led to plot a crime so carefully, so leisurely, planned that he could feel confident that detection could never follow?

Suppose that there had been an occasion when he had returned unexpectedly from his shop during the day, and found to his surprise that his flat was empty? That he had heard voices from the one below? Voices he knew? That he had waited for a long time, during which his wife had not returned to her own apartment?

Suppose that he had then gone away, unobserved as he had come, and then set a watch, and discovered that there was a regular daytime intimacy between his wife and that downstairs neighbour? Suppose he had then decided that it would be better to take a course which would remove his rival forever, rather than create a scandal by which he might lose his wife, merely transferring her to a man who had sufficient means for her support—more indeed than his own precarious financial position could assure?

There were other ways in which his suspicions might have been aroused without the knowledge of those who wronged him. A hint from a fellow tradesman who had overseen something while delivering goods. A word between the guilty pair, not meant for him, which he overheard.

There was a possible motive; but of that greed was even more strongly indicated, for a midday talk with the porter and his wife had led to disclosure of the fact that the Lovejoys were in acute financial difficulties. They were known to be pressed by tradesmen. Their Christmas rent had only been paid last week, after a distress had been levied, jeopardizing the hire-purchase furniture, which had been barely saved. Whoever had struck that cowardly unsuspected blow had put a near end to their troubles, just as it must have been seeming impossible to them that they could escape the worst experience of impecuniosity.

It did little to reduce the significance of these sinister circumstances that, while the roll-top desk had been left apparently unexplored, a small oak box which must have been kept under the bed in the adjoining room, and which had been more strongly secured, had been pulled out, its double locks forced, and its contents, consisting of miscellaneous letters and other documents, of private rather than valuable character, scattered upon the floor.

This suggested robbery as the motive of the crime, and the scattering of the papers as incidental to the search for money which might or might not have, but probably had, been there. It might have been done deliberately to mislead; but if the hand had been Edwin Lovejoy's which struck the blow, the desire for some immediate profit from his crime would have been strong enough, without any secondary motive of what he did.

The time of the murder had also been fixed within comparatively narrow limits. It must have been before the arrival of the Tuesday morning's post, for there were two letters bearing Monday night's postmark among those which were scattered upon the floor, and one of these, containing a cheque for £247 3s. 2d., as the reward of a lucky or skilful coupon which Mr. Rissole must have forwarded to a football pool on or before the previous Friday night's post, was not of the kind which a living man would have been likely to disregard.

That evidence, incidentally confirming Mrs. Lovejoy's witness as to the principal interest or occupation of the dead man, appeared to place the murder almost certainly between Friday night and Tuesday morning, which was confirmed by the medical testimony, Dr. Haliburton, the police surgeon who had appeared very promptly upon the scene, having expressed a preliminary opinion that the unfortunate man had been dead for "at least a week, and probably longer than that."

Examination of the contents of the desk had revealed evidence which appeared to fix the time within still narrower limits. The dead man had kept a diary which had every appearance of having been regularly, though not very lengthily, written up.

It was one of those books which have ruled spaces of a dozen or twenty lines for each day of the year, and for the Saturday which was almost certainly the last complete day that the man had known, there appeared this entry:

> Went out for coffee as usual, and then called to pay
> P's account. Afternoon to see Chelsea-Brentford
> match.

There was no entry for the next day. No indication that Mr. Rissole had looked over his copies of football coupons after the results of the afternoon matches had been published, and ascertained that he was a winner of something which, by the erratic course of such betting, might be anything between four-and-sixpence and four thousand pounds.

Presumably he had entered up the diary for the day when he had returned from watching the Chelsea match, and had then let in some visitor—a man almost certainly known, if not expected—by whom he had been foully stabbed in the back; unless, of course, which was a diminishing probability, the crime had not been committed until some hour of the following day.

With these facts, among others, arranging themselves in Chief Inspector Combridge's clear and experienced, if not brilliant mind, he rang the bell once again on the upmost floor.

CHAPTER V.

Mr. Lovejoy Has a Good Appetite

CHIEF INSPECTOR COMBRIDGE did not find that he was instantly admitted. He heard Mrs. Lovejoy's light steps approach the door, and had a well-founded impression that his legs were being examined cautiously through the letter-box flap. His newly acquired information upon the state of the Lovejoy finances led him to another conclusion equally sound, that this display of caution might not be directed against himself; and reflecting that the evidence of his legs alone might be inconclusive, he stepped a couple of paces back, and was rewarded by the sight of a promptly opened door.

It was not because he was in any doubt on the subject that he asked whether Mr. Lovejoy were in, for he knew that that gentleman had been followed from shop to flat less than half an hour before; but as Mrs. Lovejoy responded with a ready affirmative, and asked him in, the feeling that he was regarded as a welcome visitor came again, as it had done at his morning call. Well, that might be the lady's reaction, but would Mr. Lovejoy feel the same?

Mr. Lovejoy's feelings, whatever they might be, appeared to have left his appetite in working order. A pleasant scent of grilled mutton chops met the inspector as he entered the room, and his observant glance noted that the bones of two already eaten decorated Mr. Lovejoy's plate, while a third was in course of disappearing, and a fourth awaited its fate upon the dish before him.

The man who sat consuming this meal was sparely made, as heavy meat-eaters often are. His head was small, his features rather sharp, his hair and eyes dark, his eyebrows bushy. He was sometimes described as resembling his country's excellent Premier, at which he was pleased. At others, he suffered less complimentary comparisons.

Now his black eyes glittered upon the inspector with a sharp glance of apparent self-assurance and affability, as he excused him-

22

self for continuing his meal. He had had, he said, a hard day. After that, he came to the subject of the inspector's call with a blunt directness.

"I'm afraid," he said, "from what I hear's been going on this afternoon, that it's bad news you'll be giving us about Mr. Rissole."

Inspector Combridge considered the implications of this remark. Had the man given himself away? No, he could not fairly say that he had. The investigations which had been proceeding during the afternoon on the floor below had been conducted with extreme discretion, the body had not yet been removed, and there had been no public announcement of the murder. But the coming and going of the police-surgeon, the photographers, and other members of the force such as are attracted, like waiting vultures, to a scene of crime, could hardly have been unobserved by one so interested in the event as Mrs. Lovejoy had shown herself to be. He could not tell how audible, in this ancient house, movements on the floor below might be to one who was watching and lonely there. Short as the time had been between Mr. Lovejoy's return and his own appearance, his wife might well have given him an account of the morning calls, and of what she had heard subsequently, which would justify that remark.

Anyway, there should be no ambiguity in his reply. He prided himself on the fact that he played fair. Actually, he lacked both the subtlety of mind and the type of character which would have fitted or inclined him to deceive the criminals whom he so tenaciously followed. His method was rather that of the patient bloodhound, careful, slow, but relentless in following every twist of his victim's flight on a track which he would not leave.

If Edwin Lovejoy were an innocent man, he told him no more than he had some title to be informed, and, if he were not, no more than he already knew, when he answered: "I'm sorry to say that he's been murdered. There's no doubt about that. Stabbed in the back. I came to see what information you could give us. Mrs. Lovejoy told me that you knew him better than most."

Mrs. Lovejoy had gone into the kitchen when this was said. Her husband paused with a loaded fork half lifted towards his mouth. He exclaimed: "What a ghastly thing!" with as much show of horror, and perhaps surprise, as the occasion required, allowance being made for the fact that he was not of an emotional type.

He got up and went to the kitchen door, where the inspector heard him say: "Jane, it's bad news about Adrian. He's been murdered." And then, more faintly, with more of emotion but even less of surprise, there came his wife's reply: "What a dreadful thing!

23

Poor Adrian! But it's no more than I've said we should hear. At least, I was almost sure he was dead."

The couple re-entered the living room together and, as they did so, Mrs. Lovejoy added, half to her husband, half to the inspector: "But I don't say it's as bad as if he'd laid there ill till he died, and unable to call for help. It was that that I was so afraid about, and what made me get you to write."

"No," Inspector Combridge admitted, "perhaps not." The proposition did not invite discussion. To him, a man who died naturally was of no professional interest, whether his last hours were short or solitary, or prolonged to the latest possible second by the sedulous efforts of a surrounding group of doctors and nurses. "I was hoping," he went on, "that you might be able to give us some useful information."

"I don't know that we could," Mr. Lovejoy replied. "But you'd better tell me first what you've been able to find out, and then it'll be easier for us to say."

Inspector Combridge did not like this reply. It seemed that the man fenced with him, as innocence need not do. Yet the request was not entirely unreasonable, and he had no means of making these people speak, except upon their own terms. Showing no sign of his thoughts, he answered with apparent readiness: "Well, he'd been stabbed in the back, and almost certainly robbed. We don't know much more than that yet, though I expect we soon shall."

"How long ago should you say it was?"

"Perhaps a week, perhaps more."

A glance passed between husband and wife as this answer was given, and the woman said: "Then you'd better tell what you saw, Edwin. I'm sure it will be the better way."

Mr. Lovejoy did not appear to resent this open advice, which really gave him no option but to speak with the frankness (if that were the right word) which his wife proposed. But he was not quick to begin, and when he spoke, it was only to ask a question: "You mean it might be as far back as the Friday before last?"

Inspector Combridge was literal in his reply. Why mention the evidence—the diary in particular—which so emphatically indicated the following day, until he had heard what Mr. Lovejoy would have him believe? "The condition of the body," he answered, "is consistent with it being as far back as that."

But the ironmonger still seemed reluctant to communicate whatever was on his mind.

"I don't want," he said, "to bring trouble to an innocent man, and I'm not as clear as I should like to be that I mightn't be had up for slander. I suppose you'd guarantee me against that?"

"If you tell us in confidence any grounds for suspicion that you may have, you can rely on our discretion not to put it to any improper use."

"Well, it's no more than this. We've known Mr. Rissole for the last year, or a bit more. Been quite friendly together, and all that. And he's never seemed to have any people he knew. Just a quiet solitary man. In fact, he once told us that he'd got no near relatives, and no one to leave his money to when he died. He's said more than once that when that happened Mrs. Lovejoy would get a pleasant surprise. I'd like to think that she will, but I know people often talk like that without putting anything into writing, even when they mean what they say, so it's probably a case of 'blessed is he who expecteth nothing,' for that's precisely what she's going to get."

"There is a will which, so far as appearances go, is in order, and was only made about three months ago. It leaves everything to your wife."

"Then it's good news for us, and I don't mind telling you we can do with a bit of cash. But this isn't what I was going to say. We've got off the track somehow. It was the Friday evening before last, and the time must have been about a quarter past seven. That's almost exact, because we close at seven on Fridays, and I came straight home, as I mostly do. I met a man on the stairs—they're not very well lighted, as you can see for yourself—below Mr. Rissole's landing, whose face I didn't see clearly, but I didn't like his looks, or the way he pushed past me, as though he didn't want to be recognized.

"I thought he looked like a seaman—not naval, not neat enough for that—and a rough sort. I had a queer feeling at the time that when he saw me coming up he was half of a mind to turn back, and half to fling me to the bottom, but he just pushed past me, with his head turned away.

"I didn't think of his having been at Mr. Rissole's. I thought he'd been here, and the first thing I did when I got in was to ask what his business had been; but when I heard he hadn't called here, I saw he must have been at Mr. Rissole's below.

"When the days passed after that without Rissole being seen about, I naturally wondered if the two things had anything to do with each other, though I couldn't see what. Of course, I didn't expect anything as bad as this. In fact, if I'm frank, it was Mrs. Lovejoy who was worrying me to write. I thought it would all turn out to be nothing, more likely than not; and we should get no better thanks than busybodies usually do."

Chief Inspector Combridge considered this story. It seemed to him rather thin. In fact, just the kind that a murderer might make up to turn suspicion from his own door. He had been standing until now as one who had intended to do no more than inform these people of the fact of the tragedy of the floor below; but now he took the seat which Mrs. Lovejoy had offered when he first entered the room. He thought that there might be profit in further words than he had first intended to speak.

CHAPTER VI.

FINGERPRINTS FROM THE LOVEJOYS

"Do I understand," Inspector Combridge asked, "that you wouldn't recognize that man, if you should see him again?"

"No. I wouldn't say that exactly. I couldn't swear to his face. But I think I should know his shoulders and neck, and—well, the general shape of the man. You see, I looked at him rather closely, as far as the light and the way he pushed past me allowed."

Inspector Combridge saw that, if Mr. Lovejoy were lying, he was one who would do it with circumstance, and that he had his tale well prepared. He asked: "But you have no reason for suspecting the man, apart from the way he passed you on the stairs?"

"Not except that, and the fact that he looked a seafaring man, and we know that Rissole had been at sea, and we don't know how his money may have been made."

"I understood that he had compensation for an accidental injury."

"Yes. That's what he told us. We don't know more than that."

Inspector Combridge considered this suggestion, and believed the tale even less than before. The idea of the man who retires to enjoy money made nefariously abroad, and who is then visited by mysterious foreigners with murderous purpose—well, it may be useful to writers of the class of fiction to which it rightly belongs, but his experience had not confirmed the idea that foreigners were either more mysterious or more habitually criminal than his metropolitan neighbours, nor that those who take the way of the sea may not make their money as honestly as an ironmonger in the Hornsey Road.

It was the sort of suggestion which might appear plausible to a homebred suburban mind, and which it would be likely to put forward in the effort to turn suspicion aside. As a serious theory, Inspector Combridge had no use for it at all. But he only said: "Well, if that's all you can tell me, the man won't be very easy to find." He turned the conversation to a subject of more immediate interest to himself, by asking: "I suppose Rissole didn't always come up here—Mrs. Lovejoy told me how often he did that—you sometimes went down to him?"

"Oh yes. As much as once a week more often than not."

"I'll tell you," the inspector went on, with partial frankness, "why I'm asking you that. It's a question of fingerprints. Of course, we're making a thorough examination of the flat for any there are, and if, for instance, we should trace the seaman you saw, and find his prints where they shouldn't be, it might just be sufficient to bring the charge home to a guilty man. But as you and Mrs. Lovejoy were often there, your finger-marks may be all over the place without being any help to us.

"What I wondered was—of course, it's as you like—I've no right to ask—whether Mrs. Lovejoy and you would mind letting us have copies of yours, so that we needn't waste time over what means nothing at all."

He watched Mr. Lovejoy very closely as he asked this. What he had said was true so far that the mere presence of the fingerprints of the ironmonger and his wife in the flat of the murdered man might have no sinister significance, but the places where they would be found might give them a deadly meaning. Even so, he could have obtained them in other ways, but half his purpose had been to see how Mr. Lovejoy would respond to the proposal, the unspoken implications of which would not be lost to a guilty mind.

As to that, he did not look pleased, and his reply was not quick to come. But in the end he said, genially enough: "Well, you've brought us some good news, though I'm sorry the money comes in the way it does, and if we can save some trouble to you, I don't think we ought to refuse that. Not if Mrs. Lovejoy doesn't object." It appeared that the lady, who had been listening, more or less, to the conversation as she had been clearing the debris of her husband's meal, did not object at all. Indeed, she seemed rather childishly pleased at the idea. When a detective-sergeant arrived, with significant celerity, from the floor below, bearing the simple apparatus which the occasion required, Mrs. Lovejoy's only anxiety appeared to be that she might retain a copy of the print of her own thumb. The operation reminded her, she said, of a garden-party competition, the aim of which is to produce butterflies by folding paper over three dabs of paint.

In spite of many previous experiences of female duplicity, the official mind concluded that her own conscience was clear, not merely of complicity in Adrian Rissole's death, but of any suspicion that her husband was not equally innocent.

For the moment, he felt that he had obtained all the information that he was likely to get, and his retreat was hastened by a word from the detective-sergeant spoken aside. He said that there were County Court bailiffs upon the stairs. He had asked them to wait for a short time, so that the police might not be interrupted in a legal mission even more important than theirs. But they were becoming impatient, and could not be much longer delayed.

CHAPTER VII.

WHY MR. LOVEJOY WAS SHORT OF CASH

"IT looks to me, Combridge," Superintendent Davis concluded, when he had listened to the inspector's account of the investigations of the previous day, "to be one of those cases where the culprit will hang himself without much assistance from us."

Inspector Combridge was disposed to agree. The tale of the seafaring man might have been useful to bamboozle a jury, had there been nothing to disprove that the murder had been committed on Friday night. But with the dead man's diary providing decisive evidence that he had been alive on the next day, it might easily be so handled that it would have a contrary effect. It could be argued that this rendered the alleged incident even less credible than before; and if Edwin Lovejoy had invented something he had not seen, it was an evidence of guilty conscience which any jury would be likely to read aright.

The case might not yet be sufficiently clear to justify an arrest, but it was much to feel sure that they had their eyes on the guilty man, and encouraging to observe that he had already done so much to put the rope round his own neck. Having done so much, he might be expected to do more.

But Inspector Combridge could not accept the position with the entire complacency of his superior officer. It was not his part to sit back contentedly to watch the development of a satisfactory case. To complete that satisfaction rested with him, and he saw that there might still be difficulties upon the way.

"It doesn't follow," he said, "that the man couldn't have gone back and done Rissole in on the following day."

"No. They'll say that. We must hope that Lovejoy will try something which will put him a bit deeper in the mud than he is now. And you may learn a lot from the people on the ground floor. You've hardly begun yet."

Inspector Combridge recognized the reason of that. Considering that it was barely twenty-four hours since he had undertaken the investigation, he had little cause for dissatisfaction with the progress that he had made. The trouble was that he had been in a despondent mood. He had just failed rather badly. It was an error which a cheque drawn upon his past reputation had been sufficient to pay. But he could not afford to fail twice in succession, lest that account should be overdrawn. He was bound, for the moment, to be overcautious in all he did.

Still, so far, he had done well enough, and it seemed that fortune had been his friend. They were agreed upon that. They could have no foresight of the dilemma which lay ahead. A dilemma which, if it should not prove them wrong in their present guess, would be potent to turn their eyes to another trail, which then itself would foil them, and turn them back to that on which they already were.

"Well," he said, as he rose to go, "it's half the battle to feel that we know the criminal. It'll only be the usual grind, mugging up the proofs now."

He scarcely noticed that the telephone rang, until the superintendent called him back from a closing door, while a slow smile creased his heavy delusively somnolent features. "Show him up," he said into the instrument, and then, as he laid it down: "Funny how they never can leave the rope alone, till they've got it fixed where it ought to be. Lovejoy's here, asking to see you on urgent business."

Mr. Edwin Lovejoy, entering a moment later, certainly looked a harassed man, but he knew what he had come to say, and he lost no time. "I don't understand," he began, "what the procedure is in a case like this, but I suppose you keep possession, for a time, of what you find in the flat. That wouldn't be anything to do with me, except that you told me that there's a will in Mrs. Lovejoy's favour, and, if that's in order, it might be very important—very important indeed—if you could let my solicitor have a sight of it sometime this afternoon, and let him satisfy himself that there is really money to come."

"We shouldn't wish," the superintendent answered, "to hold the will back from whatever may be the proper direction for it to go; that is, not unless we see reason to think that it's got something to do with the crime.

"But I suppose you know that the fact that your wife may benefit doesn't give her or her solicitor any claim to take possession of it—that is, not unless she's named as executrix. How's that, Combridge?"

"The will's drawn by Mr. Jellipot, and it makes him the sole executor. "

Mr. Lovejoy received this information blankly, not being familiar with the solicitor's name, but the eyebrows of Superintendent Davis were slightly raised as he answered: "Jellipot's client, was he? Then the man who stuck that knife in him is going to be sorry for himself, if he makes it his business to hunt him down."

"I didn't suppose," the ironmonger answered, without appearing to notice the last remark, "that my wife had any claim to possess the will. It's the information I want to have as promptly as possible, as to what my wife's benefit is."

"Well," Superintendent Davis considered noncommittally, "I don't see how you can learn much today. A will isn't a document of any certain value till probate's granted, and sometimes not even then. There might be another a week later, leaving everything to a cats' home. But we'll send it round this morning to Mr. Jellipot's office—he's a solicitor in Basinghall Street—and your solicitor can get in touch with him. I dare say he'll give you any information he can; that is, if your solicitor can give a good enough reason for wanting to know."

Mr. Lovejoy was blunt in his reply: "I've got an execution in the shop, and another at home, and I can raise the money to pay them out if I get my wife's signature added to mine, and I can show that Rissole's money's coming to her."

"That's bad luck," Superintendent Davis answered slowly, "but it sounds the sort of reason that any solicitor would understand." He was studying the man closely as he spoke, wondering whether he saw a criminal who, to release himself from financial ruin, had murdered an unsuspecting friend, or one to whom a most opportune gift of fortune had come innocently, although by a tragic path. It was to learn more of the man, rather than from any interest in the event itself, that he added: "I shouldn't have said that you were quite the sort to get into a mess like that."

Mr. Lovejoy's eyes glittered with anger, either at the imputation these words conveyed, or the memories which they stirred. His cheekbones flushed darkly as he answered, giving an explanation which caused his hearers to forget that it was a probable murderer with whom they talked. More shortly than in the bitterness of his own words it may be stated that his troubles arose through a firm of multiple providers having opened a branch almost opposite the business which he had brought to a position of moderate profit by the hard work of eight previous years. He had been married no more than a few weeks when the disaster had confronted him, and from that day had fought a desperate losing battle, striving by novel methods of advertising, by the introduction of new lines of stock, by devices of window-dressing, by cutting prices, and other expedients which had only exhausted his resources more rapidly than a more passive attitude would have done, to maintain a struggle which yet moved inexorably to its certain end.

"Well," Superintendent Davis commented, when the tale was done, "it's been tough luck for you." And then he reminded himself that even tradesmen who are being ruined by a multiple store must not stab their friends in the back so that their wives may receive legacies with the promptitude which the position requires.

He added: "I shouldn't put your solicitor in touch with Mr. Jellipot, if I were you. Not at first, anyway. Go and see him yourself sometime this afternoon, and explain the jam that you're in. He might be more willing to say the right word after he'd understood what the trouble is."

Mr. Lovejoy thanked him for good advice, which he said he would take. The superintendent excused himself to his own conscience with the reflection that his advice really might be good, if the ironmonger were an innocent man; if he were not, it was as good as he deserved to get. But he knew that his real object had been to give an exceptionally astute solicitor an opportunity of studying a man who might have murdered one of his own clients.

"You might almost say," he remarked, after Mr. Lovejoy had gone, "that Rissole was murdered by Scars & Huxley's multiple stores. That is, if we're making a good guess at who handled the knife. But you'd better get to Mr. Jellipot as soon as you can. Let him have the will, and put him wise to what the position is. It'll be a pleasure to have him on our side, though I'm not saying that the case can't be handled without his help."

CHAPTER VIII.

SOME INFORMATION FROM MR. JELLIPOT

MR. JELLIPOT was a good listener. He heard the tragic tale with few interruptions, and these were no more than brief questions intended to elucidate some point on which the narrative had been less than full.

When it was done he said: "I'm sorry about Rissole. An inoffensive man, who might, I suppose, have enjoyed life for many years in his own quiet way. He had been a client of mine for longer than I have known you, Inspector. In fact, from when I had a very small practice. He was one of those clients whom it is pleasant to have—always grateful and appreciative of what you do."

It crossed Inspector Combridge's mind that if there were more lawyers as solicitous as was Mr. Jellipot for their clients' good and as indifferent to their own gain they might earn a more general gratitude from the public on whom they live. But he did not say it, for Mr. Jellipot was speaking again in his slow, hesitant manner, almost as though he were merely thinking aloud.

"As I understand, your conclusion is that the murder was committed by Edwin Lovejoy, and that he has made up the tale of the seafaring man to divert suspicion from himself?"

"Yes. That's how it looks to us."

"It would be an amazingly foolish thing to do. But I should hesitate to say that it is therefore an improbable explanation. The commission of such a murder may be taken as almost conclusive evidence of a singularly unbalanced mind. Normal prudence is not to be anticipated from such a source. So, at least, it appears to me. Yes, it has a very probable sound. But as to the existence of the seafaring man, I have to suggest that you may be wrong. Adrian Rissole had a second cousin who was a seaman. A ship's carpenter. A man named Anthony Rissole, whom, you may like to know, I could identify without difficulty He was in this office less than six months ago."

"That certainly makes it look a bit different."

"Does it? I am not sure. You will understand that I am expressing no opinion upon the guilt or innocence of a man I have never met, and whom you have described to me as a victim of circumstance rather than his own folly, in the acute commercial difficulty which he is now experiencing.

"Beyond that, I know only that my late client had a very kindly feeling towards his wife, who had shown consideration for a lonely man.

"But is it not at least possible—or even likely—that Adrian Rissole mentioned the existence of his cousin to these people of whom he saw so much during the last year? And might not have that put the idea of inventing such a visitor into the mind of a guilty man?"

"Yes. That's possible. And it brings us to the conclusion we'd already reached, only up a new road. We think the seafaring man can be ruled out. But we want to examine every possibility, all the same. I suppose you can't tell me whether the murdered man was involved in anything which might bring him in touch with the criminal world? Anything which might have made enemies for him of a dangerous kind?"

"No. I should answer with some confidence that he had none. Actually, I have seldom met a man less likely to be involved in any serious trespass against the law. I should describe him as having had a particularly simple, truthful, but singularly irresolute character."

"Suppose a young woman made love to him?"

"It is a position which I find some difficulty in visualizing. Still, it is obviously possible. He might have felt flattered. Perhaps grateful. He would certainly not have been rude. Beyond that, I cannot say what his reaction would have been likely to be. No, it is a question to which I am unable to give you a valuable reply."

"Then the next thing seems to be to look up this Tony Rissole. I suppose you don't happen to have his address?"

"Yes, I think I can give you that. But if so, it's not one where you can make a quick call, and, of course, it may have changed. If he killed Adrian Rissole, it almost certainly has. It's in New York. Twenty-Seventh Street East, if I remember rightly. I'll have it looked up for you now."

"Can you tell me whether the two men were on bad terms?"

"I shouldn't put it quite like that. Tony certainly considered he had a grievance, because an old woman, a distant relative of both, left a considerable sum of money entirely to Adrian, which Tony had expected to share.

"I believe that the trouble was that Tony's mother was of Italian origin. Unfortunately for him, he followed his mother in appearance, and the old lady said that a wop, which is, I have understood, an expression somewhat discourteous in its implications which is applied to citizens of the United States who show physical characteristics indicative of Italian blood, should not have a cent of hers.

"Anthony considered that his cousin should have ignored the will, and divided the money equally, which was somewhat further than he was prepared to go, or I could advise, and he remained acutely dissatisfied, though Adrian had assisted him more than once with substantial sums."

"A sort of dago who'd be quick with a knife?"

"I cannot say that. I have never seen him with such an article in his hand. But it is not an entirely improbable assumption. He was rather truculent on the last occasion when he was here, with the result that I told him—I told him firmly"—Mr. Jellipot repeated the word in his mildest tone—"that he would have no further advances with my consent, either large or small."

Inspector Combridge, hearing this, had no difficulty in visualizing the interview, and appreciating the baffled anger of the man who would not readily understand that the more diffident in manner Mr. Jellipot became, the more unshakable would his decision be.

"I thought," he said, "that Adrian's money came from a compensation award for a damaged leg."

"He had a pound a week from that source, which will cease now. He had a total income from other sources of nearly four pounds weekly. It was an amount which tended to increase, as he lived within his income. I may add that his money was invested with more regard to security than to the income which it would earn. If matters should prove to be otherwise in order, there is no doubt that Mrs. Lovejoy will benefit to a substantial amount."

"Yes? It seems to me that it's a rather big if."

"I must assume that your mind is on the principle of English law that a man may not benefit by his own crime. But it would be going too far to say that there are not circumstances in which his wife may. That is, if she cannot be shown to be an accessory either before or after the event. But it is a question which, we may hope, will not arise. I would prefer to meet Mr. Lovejoy this afternoon with an absolutely open mind."

"And I'd better find out a bit more about Tony Rissole."

"Yes. I think you should," Mr. Jellipot assented thoughtfully. He added: "I will instruct Newman to let you have his address as you go out. You will understand that it is a New York address, and not recent. It may be useless; but you are welcome to it, for anything it is worth."

Inspector Combridge was cheerful about that. "The New York cops," he said, "don't often let us down, if we start them on the right trail. But I don't say it was him. I just want to be sure he wasn't about, and then we'll give Mr. Lovejoy a chance of telling a jury it wasn't him."

Mr. Jellipot, either because he was too much distressed by the. inspector's regrettable grammar, or because he approved the indicated programme, made no answer to this, and the interview terminated.

Inspector Combridge left with the determination, in a spirit of routine thoroughness, to eliminate Tony Rissole before proceeding to the extremity of applying for a warrant for Edwin Lovejoy's arrest; but he did not overlook the possibility which Mr. Jellipot had put into his mind. If Adrian Rissole had talked of his cousin, perhaps indicating his character unfavourably, and implying that there was little friendship between them, which in view of the admitted intimacy which had existed between himself and his upstairs neighbours was at least probable, it would have been sufficient to originate the idea of the "seafaring man," even had it not been likely, apart from that, to come to the mind of a murderer aware of Adrian's antecedents, and having had a full week's leisure in which to prepare his tale.

If that were so, the C.I.D. would be fooled indeed if they should allow themselves so easily to be turned aside.

CHAPTER IX.

Mr. Jellipot Consults His Clerk

MR. JELLIPOT had lunch served in his own room, as he would often do when pressure of business was heavy. It was understood that he was not to be disturbed at such times, unless the occasion should be extreme.

While he consumed the cold meat and cheese which was the simple fare he preferred at that time of day, he took the opportunity to review the various matters he had on hand with the patient thoroughness of a methodical mind.

Now the murder of which he had just heard occupied his thoughts to the exclusion of the provisions of a most complicated will on which they should have been more profitably engaged. Mr. Balker's abstruse intentions would receive sufficient consideration, if necessary during the night hours; but Adrian Rissole was a man whom he had known for many years, though only as an occasional client. He had been drawn into cases of criminal homicide against his will more than once before, and had defended those who had not all been guiltless with a success which certainly had not vexed his mind.

But now he had been introduced to murder from a different angle: almost—for his imagination was singularly vivid when it had realities with which to deal—from that of the one who can never be present when such inquisitions are held. He saw the long years of placid contented life, the uncounted days, the innumerable minutes of sentient existence, of which Adrian Rissole had been irretrievably robbed by that one pitiless thrust. Indignation stirred him to articulate speech. "It is a matter," he informed his empty room in a mild voice, "on which no peradventure should be allowed." His voice sank to an even quieter note as he added: "It should be resolved beyond doubt." His thoughts were on Anthony Rissole, whom he did, and Edwin Lovejoy, whom he did not, know. On the information he had, it seemed that it was between them that the law must choose.

His knowledge of Tony Rissole inclined him to think him the guilty man, but he rebuked this presumption with the thought that he was one whom he did not like. And he saw that, if Tony were innocent, there was probability that he would have been sufficiently far from the scene of the crime to prove it beyond dispute.

But the case against Edwin Lovejoy was widely different. He saw that, at its weakest, it was not without the maximum indications both of motive and opportunity. These may not be proof, even in conjunction, however strong, but they are pointers which will most often cause the light of enquiry to be directed upon the guilty man. And the inferences which might be drawn therefrom would become far stronger if it should appear probable that the vision of the seafaring man was no better than a concocted tale. It might even be held to go far in justifying the police should they arrest and thereby require him to prove his innocence, which, as the law regarding the giving of evidence by accused persons is now interpreted, is the actual result of putting a man on trial upon a capital charge.

But the immediate question was how he should receive Mr. Lovejoy, or his solicitor, during the afternoon. He saw that the time for reflection would not be long, for the intended application was not of a nature to be delayed. The interval of his customary seclusion had not ended when he picked up the telephone and summoned his managing clerk from the outer office.

"Newman," he said, "here is Adrian Rissole's will, which Inspector Combridge brought this morning."

"Nothing wrong, sir, I hope?"

"Nothing wrong with the will. Mr. Rissole was murdered a week ago."

Newman, a neat young man, with a faint suggestion of Hebrew origin in his intelligent face, and a habit of unobtrusive efficiency which his employer approved, took this information quietly, though there was some evidence of feeling in his voice as he answered: "I'm sorry to hear that, sir. He wasn't the sort of man you'd expect to get into any trouble. It seems queer we hadn't heard earlier."

"Yes. It has only just been discovered. You would feel confident that he had not made any later testamentary dispositions?"

"Yes, sir. Not without letting us know. We could feel sure of that."

"So I think. Then we shall answer any enquiry frankly, but exactly, that we are satisfied that the will is in order, and has not been superseded."

Edward Newman received this instruction with his usual intelligence. He saw that there was more that he might be told, but it was not his habit to ask for more than his employer gave. He only asked: "We are not to say that we expect that it will be admitted for probate?"

"No. It will be better that it should not be put in that way. Nor, of course, to the contrary. It is a matter on which we have no need to express any opinion."

"Yes, sir. That will be all?"

"Not quite. I believe you sometimes saw Rissole outside business hours?"

"Yes, sir. I just saw him. He used to drop in at the Black Eagle. He liked watching the darts there on Saturday nights."

"That was the only day of the week?"

"I couldn't say that. No doubt others could. I don't go myself except when there's a match there."

"You probably noticed his absence last Saturday?"

"No, sir. We were playing away."

Mr. Jellipot was slightly surprised. "You mean," he asked, "that you are a member of a team which engages regularly in this popular sport?"

Mr. Newman had occasion to observe the erratic limits of human fame. There are probably not more than two men in the south of England who can throw a dart with such accuracy as he, and one of these requires three strong whiskies before his hand becomes steady enough to display his skill. He said: "Yes, sir. I play a little."

"Then I have no doubt that I can congratulate you on playing a good game. But, on the Saturday before, was he there then?"

"I could scarcely say that with certainty. No, I believe not."

"But you are not sure? It might be a most important point."

"I shouldn't be prepared to swear that he wasn't there." He paused a moment, recollecting the occasion. "I could swear that I didn't see him. He used always to sit in one corner. I could say that he wasn't there for most of the time between seven and nine."

"Which he usually was?"

"Yes. Like a fixture."

"You would have spoken to him if he had been there?"

"Just to say good evening. Perhaps a word or two more. Nothing beyond that."

"You never met Mr. Lovejoy?"

"I don't recognize anybody by that name."

Mr. Jellipot approved the careful limitation of this reply. Newman might have seen a dozen men in the bar parlour of the Black Eagle without knowing the names they bore.

"He is an ironmonger in the Hornsey Road. He and his wife occupy the flat above that in which Rissole lived."

"Isn't it a Mrs. Lovejoy who benefits by the will?"

"Yes. The wife. Combridge suspects the husband of the murder."

"Not the lady, sir?"

"He thinks it may have been with her knowledge. But more probably not. It is unlikely that she struck the blow. Edwin Lovejoy is coming to see me any moment now. Or I may hear from his solicitors. But he is more likely to come."

As Newman made no comment on this information, Mr. Jellipot went on: "It is not a matter of undertaking his defence for a crime with which he is not yet charged, which, under any circumstances, I should emphatically refuse. But Mr. Lovejoy has his own solicitors. He wants to arrange with them for an immediate advance on Mrs. Lovejoy's expectations under the will."

"Yes, sir? He isn't losing much time."

"I understand that he is in acute financial difficulties."

This statement also being received in expressionless silence, Mr. Jellipot added: "We must, of course, assume nothing. Many people of excellent character are short at times of adequate financial resources in a sufficiently liquid form."

"Yes, sir. Of course."

"There is no one whom your slight knowledge of Rissole would cause you to suspect?"

"I might have thought of the cousin, sir. That is, if he'd been anywhere around."

"So did I. Mr. Lovejoy says that he saw someone whom he describes as a seafaring man leaving Rissole's flat about the time of the murder."

"Well, sir, if anyone else saw him?"

"Yes. It is a point on which Inspector Combridge is sure to make very thorough enquiries."

"Yes, sir. He's not one to miss much."

Mr. Jellipot agreed: "He has qualities which we, who cannot hope to emulate, must be content to admire."

Newman withdrew to the door, and then turned to say: "I rather think Mr. Lovejoy's here now, sir."

"Very well. Have him shown in at once."

The next moment, Edwin Lovejoy entered the room.

CHAPTER X.

A Surprising Action by Mr. Jellipot

SUNK in the comfortable chair at the left of the solicitor's desk, Mr. Lovejoy came to his point with the same directness which he had shown to his previous auditors. He found Mr. Jellipot to be a patient listener to a tale which he had heard little more than an hour before. But, beyond that, he was not helpful. His voice was toneless, his attitude semi-detached.

It was an attitude too colourless to be felt as hostile, but Mr. Lovejoy became aware that he was not sympathetically received.

"You have told your solicitors," Mr. Jellipot asked at last, "that you would be calling upon me?"

"Yes, I gave them a look in just before lunch."

"You would like me to give you a letter addressed to them?"

"I should be very much obliged."

"Very well, I will do that."

Mr. Jellipot rang for a stenographer. He asked, as the young lady entered: "Your solicitors are?"

"Jones & Snelpit, New Bedford Alley."

Mr. Jellipot accepted the information in his previous expressionless manner. In any case, it was no business of his. He dictated:

Re Adrian Rissole, deceased.

I am writing at the request of Mr. Edwin Lovejoy to inform you of the existence of a will dated—(Mr. Newman will supply you with that)—and duly executed by the above deceased, under which Mrs. Alice Lovejoy, described as of 4, Barclay Buildings, S.W.1, is the sole beneficiary, to an amount which, to the best of my present knowledge, is likely to be somewhat over four thousand pounds.

Writing as the sole executor of the said will, I may add that I see no reason to doubt that it represents the final testamentary dispositions of the above deceased.

Yours Faithfully,

E. E. Jellipot

Mr. Jellipot's telephone had already sounded its summoning note as he finished this short dictation. He said, as he picked up the receiver: "Let me have it for signature as soon as it has been typed. Mr. Lovejoy will take it with him," but then, as he heard the name of those who had rung up, he added "You'd better wait a moment, Miss Gill. Yes, Mr Jellipot speaking."

"This is Jones & Snelpit," he heard. "Isaac Snelpit speaking. We understand that you will be acting in connection with the estate of Adrian Rissole."

"Yes."

"You'll be having a man named Lovejoy calling on you this afternoon—"

"He is with me now."

"He says you've got a will by which a pot of money comes to his wife."

"Adrian Rissole left his whole estate to Mrs. Alice Lovejoy."

"Then it's all O.K.? We thought we'd rather have it from you direct."

"The will was drawn in this office about six months ago. I can vouch for it having been duly executed."

"Yes. There's another point that we're bound to look at. There's the point of who bumped Rissole off, as the Yankees say. We know you're in with the police on this. We'd like just a word from you of the right sort."

"You appear to have been seriously misinformed. I am not acting, nor expecting to act, in any capacity whatever, except as executor of the will."

"But you could give us the right tip all the same?"

Mr. Jellipot was slow to reply. When he spoke it was with unusual deliberation, even for him: "I do not profess to misunderstand you. It may be a natural question for you to raise. But it is one on which I can express no opinion."

"But you'd know if the police—"

"I am sorry. I can express no opinion at all."

Mr. Jellipot cut off with some abruptness. He had been aware that Mr. Lovejoy watched him with anxious eyes. He knew that what he had said would have rendered it impossible to obtain the advance so urgently needed, or—more probably, Jones & Snelpit being what they were—that it would be made on the most onerous terms that the law allowed, or that the extremity of Edwin Lovejoy's necessity could induce him to undertake. And having done this, he was not entirely easy in mind.

"You can leave that letter, Miss Gill, unless I ring for it to be done." Having given this instruction, he turned to his anxious visitor. There were things in his mind which would not be pleasant but which a fine sense of honour might constrain him to say. Or he might see a stronger reason for saying less. Timidly tenacious, he started at some distance from a point which he was no less certain to reach.

"You've known Jones & Snelpit a good while?"

"No. I went to Gordon Montague, the moneylender, last week. There was no other way by which I could hope to get through. And he sent me to them. He said, if they advised a loan, it could be arranged. Of course, that was before we'd any idea of this money coming the way it has."

"No other way?" Mr. Jellipot thought. It seemed that another had been found, by whatever hand. He asked: "You will have grasped the purport, more or less, of the conversation, one side of which you have just heard?"

"Not very well, I'm afraid."

"Your solicitors put a question to me to which I do not know the answer—and had I been more fully informed, it is improbable that I should have been free to gratify their curiosity." After a moment's pause, Mr. Jellipot, being scrupulous in verbal equity, even towards those whom he did not approve, added: "But perhaps curiosity is an inappropriate word. It may be considered to be a question material to the security of the transaction which is proposed."

As he spoke, he looked at a man whose perturbation, from whatever cause it might arise, was beyond concealment. "You mean I shan't be able to get the advance?"

"I am not aware that I expressed any opinion on that point, nor that I should be asked to give it. But I should suppose that, if you obtain the accommodation which you require, it may be on very onerous terms."

"I said last week that I'd pay anything up to twenty percent for a hundred pounds to tide me over till I could realize on some stock that I may get another firm to take off my hands. I hoped to get it in time to save what's been happening during the last few days. But I reckon ten percent ought to be enough now, with Mrs. Lovejoy's signature added to mine. But I can't get them to say anything definite. I couldn't last week, and I can't now. Only I understood this morning that there'd be some cash in sight if I could get this letter from you."

"It is not for me," Mr. Jellipot answered, with professional propriety uppermost in his mind, "to express any opinion as to the terms on which your legal advisers will be able to negotiate the accommodation which you have instructed them to arrange. But if ten percent per annum were in your mind, I am afraid that substantial revision of that—"

Mr. Lovejoy interrupted with some impatience, for which he had the excuse that his affairs were urgent, and it was difficult to see how these depressing opinions could help his need. "Well," he said, "I don't see why they shouldn't. Anyway, I've got to hear what they say. If they were willing to talk about helping me last week, I don't see why there should be much dallying now. I thought the letter sounded all right. If you'll be kind enough to let me have that—"

"Yes. You can have that." But having given this assurance, Mr. Jellipot made no motion towards the telephone through which the instruction to type it must be conveyed. He sat for some moments in thought, as though ignoring the existence of the anxious man at his side.

He was in no doubt as to the course which he would take. He paused only to examine the origins of his knowledge, the circumstance of the official confidence he had received, and the degrees to which either honour or etiquette should restrain his lips. He was still unsure whether he were in the company of a heartless criminal or a man whose financial crisis was to be relieved by a tragic chance; but, guilty or not, he was surely entitled to understand the suspicion under which he lay, and the nature of the obstacle to his obtaining a loan on the easy terms which he had expected to gain.

Relieved of restraining doubts, Mr. Jellipot moved obliquely towards the explanation which he had determined to give, as diffident courtesy, and a radical doubt as to the character of Edwin Lovejoy, impelled him to do.

"You will readily understand—you are, indeed, doubtless aware—that there are a variety of circumstances under which the provisions of a will may fail to materialize to the benefit of those who are mentioned therein, or to the extent which its terms express?"

"You mean that there's a snag that the letter didn't mention, and that Jones & Snelpit have nosed out?"

The man spoke now in a voice of sharp anxiety. He had forgotten his impatience to go.

"No. I meant less than, or somewhat differently from, that. At least, I should have expressed it another way.

"I was merely generalizing on that which must be obvious to any intelligent mind. A will may not be properly executed. It may be superseded by one of a later date. It may purport to dispose of property which does not exist; or has been subsequently alienated from the disposition of the testator, or will be consumed in the discharge of unsuspected liabilities of the deceased. The testator may not have been of sound mind when he made the will.

"These are the routine risks of anyone who advances money upon an expectation of such a kind. In the present instance, I do not think that any of them need give you an anxious hour.

"But there are others which are equally serious, but more improbable—more remote. There is a provision of English law which prohibits any man from profiting by his own crime."

"Well, that sounds right enough. But what's the one that's going to make trouble for us?"

Mr. Lovejoy, as he asked this, looked genuinely puzzled. Mr. Jellipot knew that if he could gauge the authenticity of that bewilderment he would know at least half of that which the police were concerned to prove. But that was beyond his power. Would a guilty man be able to control himself to such blankness of incomprehension? Or would an innocent one be so slow to grasp the fact that the circumstances of Adrian Rissole's death brought suspicion inevitably to his own door? They were questions which he must ask himself without obtaining any certain reply.

He said quietly: "If you consider the circumstance surrounding the murder, and the fact that Mrs. Lovejoy is the one—the only one—who benefits from it, you will see that, however unfortunate or unfair it may be to you, it suggests a possibility which anyone contemplating an advance upon Mrs. Lovejoy's expectation must, almost inevitably, observe."

There was no doubt that Mr. Lovejoy understood now. His black eyes glowed with anger. His face reddened to the neck. "You're as good as telling me that I killed Adrian. Or perhaps" — his voice changed to a rasping sarcasm—"you'd make out that Mrs. Lovejoy did it herself. I think it's a monstrous thing! Why, it as we who put the police on to it, or he'd be lying there now, it's about ten chances to one."

Mr. Jellipot was unimpressed by this outburst. "If," he said, "you had listened with even moderate attention to what I said, you must have known that I made no accusation against either Mrs. Lovejoy or yourself, which it is not my business to do."

Mr. Lovejoy controlled himself to say: "I beg your pardon. That was how it sounded to me."

"I merely warned you that there is a theoretical possibility which such a firm as Jones & Snelpit—towards whom this verbal construction must not be taken to imply anything which is unsaid—would be unlikely to overlook."

"You mean that they're a low lot? Well, it makes no difference now. If they thought that—and they must have been spitting it out to you over the phone—I wouldn't take any money from them as a gift. Not if it meant saving the shop. And I know that Jane will feel just the same."

He seemed to be stirred by his own words to a second fury of indignation. He rose abruptly as he spoke. Mr. Jellipot was again unsure whether he watched an exhibition of genuine feeling or a well-acted part.

"Your feeling may be natural," he said, with little cordiality in his voice, "but you would, I think, be wiser to consider the position in a calmer mood."

"I'm not going to them now, if you mean that."

"It is not a course which, under any circumstances, I should have advised, and I am consequently unlikely to urge you to do so, though it would have been outside my province to interfere. But you will observe that I might have answered their enquiry in a way which would have disposed them to assist you more readily than they would now be likely to do."

"You mean you think the same thing!"

"No. In your own word, it would be monstrous, on any knowledge I have, to accuse you of such a crime. But Messrs. Jones & Snelpit assumed that I was acting for the police, which was a mistake, and therefore that I could give them assurances which were beyond my power."

Mr. Lovejoy sat down again. "You mean the police—?" he began, and stopped. There was a note of incredulity in his voice, but his colour had changed to a mottled pallor. "You don't really mean that they think we'd be capable of a thing like that?"

"I mean nothing which I have not said. I hope very sincerely that the truth will be discovered in such a way that you will be relieved of any further anxiety."

Mr. Lovejoy rose again. "Well, you've given me something to think of I didn't expect to hear." He said this with a scowl, and there was no gratitude in his voice. It was with an obvious effort that he added: "But I dare say that you've meant it well."

He half held out his hand, and then withdrew it, either from unwillingness to exchange a handshake with one who had voiced such an accusation, or, more probably, in doubt of whether he might not be met with a disconcerting rebuff.

Certainly Mr. Jellipot made no corresponding motion. He asked, as though seeing nothing and oblivious of what he heard: "What do you propose to do to satisfy the executions of which you have told me?"

"I don't feel that I care much if they sell me up."

"It is," Mr. Jellipot spoke as one who contemplates abstract truth, "a wasteful process, of which I seldom approve."

"When I left this morning there was two pound three in the till. You can't do much with that."

"It is normally possible, if it should have my recommendation, to secure an advance of moderate amount against such expectations from a respectable bank."

Mr. Lovejoy stared incredulously "You mean you'd recommend it, after what you've said?"

"It would not be a matter for which you should thank me at all. I have to consider that it is what my client might have wished me to do."

"I suppose you'll want me to bring Mrs. Lovejoy here?"

"No, I think not."

The suggestion had brought an almost frightened look to Mr. Jellipot's face. Was he to have some intolerably pathetic woman, in three days' time, begging him to undertake the defence of a guilty man? There were few people in London whom he would be more reluctant to meet.

"No," he repeated. "We can do rather better than that. You are on the telephone at your home address? Mrs. Lovejoy would most likely be there?"

"Considering she's got a man sitting all the time on the kitchen chair—"

"I'm afraid she must risk leaving him in the flat. You can phone her from here to be at the High Holborn branch of the London & Northern Bank within half an hour, or as near to that as a taxi can get her there. If necessary, she must ring at the side door. Meanwhile, I will send a clerk with you who will arrange the matter in the customary manner. No, it is a purely business affair. You should not thank me at all."

CHAPTER XI.

THE BANKER IS PLEASED TO LEND

MR. NEWMAN, accompanying Mr. Lovejoy to the High Holborn branch of the London & Northern Bank, his eyes observant, and his lips only opening for such casual interchanges as the incidents of the short journey required, concluded that he sat beside a man who was well content.

So it was. The indignation, real or assumed, with which Edwin Lovejoy had met the suggestion that he might be suspected of the crime appeared to have passed away.

He may have accepted Mr. Jellipot's unexpected offer as evidence of the solicitor's confidence in his own innocence, as most men would.

He may, beyond that, have taken it for proof that Mr. Jellipot knew him to be unsuspected by the police.

He may have drawn some subordinate satisfaction from the fact that Mr. Isaac Snelpit awaited a client who would not come.

He had, at least, the confident expectation that his immediate financial troubles would be relieved, and that on better terms than he could have expected an hour before.

Arriving at the bank, they were shown without delay into the manager's office.

Mr. Rutland, a man of good sense, but with some pomposity of manner, received his new client with cordiality, a telephone call from Mr. Jellipot having already acquainted him with the essential facts of the case, and the probable extent of the accommodation required. Mr. Jellipot was the trusted solicitor of the bank, and his word was not lightly to be disregarded.

In this instance, he had taken all responsibility from the bank manager's shoulders. He had made no mention of the suspicions which might attach to Mr. or Mrs. Lovejoy, or the possible legal consequences of a successful prosecution, though he had, of course, mentioned the tragic circumstance from which the lady was expected to benefit; but he had added: "As I am the executor of Adrian Rissole's will, I am sending you a letter accepting responsibility for any advance you may make up to £300, prior to probate being granted."

Mr. Rutland might be slightly surprised, but it was not his business to question so satisfactory an assurance. A bank makes its profit by lending money. When it can do so without risk, it may have little curiosity concerning the motives of those who guarantee a hazard it would be slower to undertake. And Mr. Jellipot had the reputation of having good reason for what he did.

Mr. Rutland occupied the time until Mrs. Lovejoy arrived by enquiring the extent of the immediate accommodation required. He spoke of a joint account, but prudently avoided suggesting that that of the ironmongery business should be transferred to his own bank, until he had gained further experience of the position. It was too probable that there would he an existing overdraft there!

In stating the nature and extent of his liabilities, Mr. Lovejoy became blunt and bitter, in a tone which Mr. Rutland approved. He gave an impression of telling the whole truth, which, on such occasions, is rarely done.

The executions which were now levied would require £57 for their discharge, including their mounting costs.

Other urgent payments would absorb nearly £100. Possibly quite that figure.

Mr. Rutland proposed an overdraft of £200. "If you should require rather more, you must see me again."

He felt that he had carried out Mr. Jellipot's instructions, and protected his interests. More always *was* required in such instances. It would have been a mistake to offer too readily the outside figure which his instructions allowed.

Mrs. Lovejoy arrived in some natural excitement. It was a mood which showed her limited physical attractions at their best. Mr. Rutland shook hands benignly. He thought her a pretty girl. Her eyes sparkled. After the experiences of the past year, with its increasing stringencies, its ever-narrowing credit, its acuter worries in recent weeks, it was pleasant to think that present money was available, and that there would be more in the days to be.

It means much to a woman to know that tradesmen will be obsequious again. She could not be hardly condemned if she gave little thought to a dead man from whose kindness her rescue came. She thought of suede shoes which she would buy before 6:30 tonight, after which it would be no longer desirable to keep her feet as far as possible under the table.

She watched Mr. Rutland fill in the blanks of a printed form which he required her to sign. She wrote her full name. Then her specimen signature on a separate slip. She was impressed by the importance of what she did.

Finally, a cheque book was supplied. A cheque drawn and signed. Mr. Rutland touched his bell. A clerk entered, took out the cheque, and returned with banknotes and cash. Eighty-five pounds lay on the table. Her husband made no motion, giving her the pleasure of picking it up.

Edward Newman, watching her with a very dubious mind, inclined to the same opinion that Chief Inspector Combridge had formed, that she had a conscience at happy ease; but he too reflected what good actresses women are. Of Edwin Lovejoy he was even less sure. He judged him to be a man of alert wits, and of some bitterness against a world which had not been kind to him. He had been obstinate, desperate, in a struggle which he would not resign. He might be ruthless under such stress: one whom fine scruples would not retard. Even one who, to avoid shameful defeat, would go to the length of cunningly plotted crime. Was it possible that the letter to Scotland Yard of which he had heard from Mr. Jellipot had been prompted not only by strategic considerations of his own safety, but to hasten the moment when this urgent relief could be obtained?

It must have been exceptionally exasperating to have the bailiffs about the door if he knew that the will which made his wife a moderately affluent woman lay undiscovered and inoperative with the dead man on the floor below!

They left the bank together, and Mr. Newman said that, with Mr. Lovejoy's permission, he would accompany them home. It had been Mr. Jellipot's instruction to him that he should render any desired assistance in discharging the executions.

Mr. Lovejoy accepted this offer with as gracious a manner as it was his habit to show. Mr. Newman signalled to a passing taxi. Mrs. Lovejoy, who did not often enter such vehicles, felt that the pleasures of wealth were already hers.

They drove first to the shop, where Mr. Newman quickly disposed of an unwelcome occupant of the rear office, and then to the flat, where a similar clearance was made with the same professional brevity. As the man slouched out, Mrs. Lovejoy pushed up the kitchen window.

"He wasn't such a bad sort," she said, "in his own way. Said he'd just lost an aunt from Bright's Disease, whatever that is, and was worried because he thought he'd got some of the same symptoms. If it has anything to do with getting soaked, I should say he's heading the right way. Anyhow, I shall feel better when we've got some fresh air." She invited Mr. Newman to stay to tea, which he was willing to do.

Eating buttered toast in this atmosphere of hospitable familiarity, it was hard to think of these two everyday people as being guilty of a sordid and cruel crime. Hard—and rather dreadful—to think that one or both of them might soon be feeling a rope adjusted around the neck, to die without receiving—or deserving—sympathy from a hostile world. They were happy now, animated in the relief which had come so promptly, and through a better channel than they had expected. Or, at least, the woman appeared to be so, without any qualifying doubt. The man seemed at times almost as light-hearted as she; but at others he would seem to rouse himself with conscious effort from a gloomier mood. Was there meaning in that?

Edward Newman would have preferred to think not, but judgment was more dubious than inclination. He had no wide experience of criminal character, for Mr. Jellipot's practice was mainly in civil matters. But he had heard it said that murderers are not outwardly different from their fellow men. They kiss their children. They say: "Haven't you passed me the wrong cup? I'm sure there's more than one lump in this," in the most natural manner, as Mr. Lovejoy was doing now. Actually, the two murderers with whom he had come into previous professional contact had been pleasant people, easy to like.

But their murders had been of a different order from this; they had not been sordid, treacherous, mean, as this surely was.

He reflected that Mr. Jellipot appeared to be giving the Lovejoys his support. While that was so, loyalty to his employer constrained him to the same attitude. And there was more than routine loyalty in the confidence he felt in any course which Mr. Jellipot might take. "The old man," he thought, "doesn't often go wrong." But, on the other hand, the solicitor's actions were not always of the obvious kind.

He thought, as he rose to go, that the conversation between the two during the following ten minutes would almost certainly be of a revealing quality. The doubt of whether it might be possible to turn back and listen at the door entered his mind, but was not entertained. He felt that it would transgress the ethics of a particularly respectable solicitor's office. Yet he supposed that Chief Inspector Combridge would do such things without hesitation should the opportunity arise. He did not condemn, but preferred to think that his own weekly £6 15s. and extras came to him by other means. And he concluded philosophically that if he had decided to look and listen through the letter slit in the door, he might have found that he could hear little and see less.

"You'll let me know," he said, "if you get any more trouble—summonses, I mean, and things like that. You can't be too quick in such matters, if you wish to keep down the costs."

Mr. Lovejoy said he certainly would, though he thought there wouldn't be much more of that sort of thing now. He shook hands with warmth, for him.

So did Mrs. Lovejoy. Her parting words were warm also, with a gratitude that her eyes confirmed.

CHAPTER XII.

THE TENANTS ON THE GROUND FLOOR

MR. NEWMAN considered that the afternoon was too far advanced for it to be worthwhile to go back to the office, where he had left nothing undone which could not wait till the next day. Not being in the habit of using taxis for his private affairs, he stood for a moment upon the edge of the pavement, debating what bus would serve his homeward purpose best, and in which direction to seek it.

As he did so, he observed Inspector Combridge approaching, and without turning his head again was aware that he had entered the porchway of Barclay Buildings. He supposed that the inspector sought a further interview with the suspected couple, and concluded that, had he been foolish enough to stoop to the keyhole, he would have been interrupted from the rear in that inglorious attitude. It showed the folly of what he had never seriously intended to do.

Actually, he was mistaken. Inspector Combridge went no further than the ground floor.

Both observing the other, neither had supposed himself to have been observed, nor that there was any importance in his having noticed the other's presence. Yet there was to be one momentous consequence. For when next morning Inspector Combridge was discussing with Superintendent Davis the information which he had obtained by this visit to Barclay. Buildings, he mentioned casually: "I saw Jellipot's clerk leaving as I went in. He must have been at the Lovejoys'. That's a safe guess."

Superintendent Davis looked serious. "If that means Jellipot's taking up their defence—"

"I don't see that it does. We sent the man to his office."

"Only so that he could give him a letter, and have a chance of telling us whether he thought him a guilty man. I don't see why that should take his clerk to the flat. I suppose you told him the whole case, so far as we've got it now?"

"Yes. More or less. But we got something from him. It was he who put us on to Rissole's cousin."

"Who'll probably prove to have been at sea...."

"Well, we'll soon know that. If it turns out that he was here at the time, he'll have my vote for the dock."

"You think that's more likely than that Lovejoy made up the tale about meeting someone on the stairs?"

"I don't say that. I said *if*. I'm just doubtful between the two."

"You told Jellipot about the diary?"

"No. I don't think I mentioned that. Nor to the Lovejoys. I know I didn't to them. I'd got a feeling that that might do us most good as a surprise when we've picked the man, and he's spit out whatever lie he wants to make a jury believe."

"Well, if you haven't mentioned it to Jellipot, I don't think I should now."

Chief Inspector Combridge agreed easily. He didn't think that the solicitor intended to take on the Lovejoys' defence, and he knew him well enough to see the extreme improbability of his exerting himself in such a direction before any charge had been made against them. But he knew the value of silence. The reticence merely became deliberate which had been instinctive before; but this probably turned the scale between silence and speech in the conversation of a later day, and so deflected the course of events.

"Remember the Porson murder?" he asked, his mind reverting to his visit to the ground floor of Barclay Buildings, from which he had been momentarily diverted, and where he had come on an unexpected and somewhat disconcerting fact, which must extend enquiries to a third direction, and yet might be of no relevance whatever.

Superintendent Davis said that he did, which was not surprising, for it was his conduct of that notorious case which had secured him promotion to the position he now enjoyed.

"Yes," he said. "What of that?"

"Harry Vestman's living on the ground floor of Barclay Buildings."

"Sure there's no mistake? I thought he cleared off to America."

"So he did. He was quite frank about that, and so was the woman, when they found I remembered them too well to make denial worthwhile. He's got the woman with him who used to call herself Jimmy's wife. They've taken the name of Aide—Mr. and Mrs. Aide—now. Says it was his grandmother's, and he went to America, and changed it while he was there, because he didn't like to be pointed at as one who'd been charged with murder, and whose brother had been hanged, however innocent he'd been."

"Lucky'd be a better word."

"Well, if a jury say a man's innocent, we can't go beyond that."

Superintendent Davis rarely allowed any expression of emotion, unless it were a faint flicker of humour in half-shut eyes, to appear on his heavy features, but there was some evidence of annoyance now, as he answered: "That wasn't quite what happened. You ought to remember better than that. We withdrew the case against him. The evidence wasn't strong enough, with him having an alibi which we couldn't upset. If we'd tried to get them both convicted, a jury might have been fools enough to let them both go. So we put Jim in the dock alone, and made sure of him. But Harry was just as guilty as he. What does he say that he's doing now?"

"Got a shop in Dean Street. Cheap gown. He and the woman run it together. Of course, we must check that, but it's probably true. If they'd gone on with their old games, we should have run across them before now."

The superintendent agreed upon the soundness of that deduction. It is not often that those whom Scotland Yard regards as criminals who have escaped the due penalty of their misdeeds elude its subsequent observation, and the man and woman who had made reluctant admission of their identity under the pressure of Inspector Combridge's retentive memory were not of the kind to be easily overlooked.

The man had almost certainly been his brother's companion in a burglary which had resulted in the brutal murder of an elderly lady who had surprised the thieves. Jim Vestman, betrayed by a receiver to whom he had offered some of the dead woman's jewellery, had been convicted and hanged on convincing though entirely circumstantial evidence, countered only by an ineffectual alibi; the woman who had then called herself his wife, and was now living with his brother on the same basis, having sworn that he had been with her during the night.

But Harry Vestman's alibi had been of better quality, and the evidence against him much weaker. It was a case where the police knew much which could not be offered in evidence, including the past records of the two men, who had worked inseparably together in previous crimes of a similar kind.

But neither of them had been previously convicted, though they had been unsuccessfully charged. On the official records, they were entered as the almost certain perpetrators of a similar murder three years earlier. The police regarded them as particularly cunning and ruthless criminals, and it had been no small satisfaction to see one pass into the hangman's hands, though the other had wriggled free.

"Of course they said they knew nothing about it?"

"Not exactly. They said they knew nothing about the murder, of course. But when I pressed them as to what they had observed about Rissole's habits, or who they might have seen him with, they brought up the same tale as Lovejoy. They'd seen a seaman go up to his flat about a fortnight ago, or perhaps less, but they couldn't say which day of the week it was."

"How did they know he was going up to Rissole's flat?"

"Because they knew the man. They say they'd seen him walking out with Rissole before."

"Then they could identify him?"

"Yes. So they say. Though they're not the kind of witnesses you'd choose to put into the box. But they both say they could. They say he was a foreign-looking man. Probably dago. It's evident, for what it's worth, that it's Tony Rissole they've seen about."

"To an extent, it confirms Lovejoy's tale?"

"I'm not sure that it does. Not to help to let Lovejoy out I mean. It goes to prove that Tony used to call at the flat, but we knew that from Jellipot already. If Lovejoy or Vestman did the murder, they'd either of them be glad to throw suspicion on Rissole's cousin. If Tony did it, we can suppose that the Vestmans and Lovejoy are all telling the truth. If either of them did it, then the other is telling the truth much more likely than not.

"That's how it looks to me, and it may be useful when we've got other evidence, and decided who to charge; but it doesn't seem to help us much in that direction. We've just got three suspects now, instead of two.

"But there's one point that may prove to be of some importance. They say they can't be sure which day it was they saw Tony last, but it wasn't a Saturday. It might have been any weekday except that. They say they were coming home together, and they saw the man enter the building before them. That puts it at between six and seven P.M., and rules out Saturday, because that day the woman comes home separately at one o'clock, and the man stays on to write up the books."

"That sounds rather as though they're telling the truth."

"Yes. Perhaps it does. But how far does it take us? Say they *did* see Tony going upstairs. Say that it was the Friday that Lovejoy says that he saw him too. It doesn't prove more than that the man called. It isn't a crime for a cousin to do that. It doesn't even show that he was let in. Adrian might have been dead before that, and Tony knocked and gone away. Or he may have left him alive, and he may have been murdered by someone else on the next day. As a matter of fact, we know by the diary that it was the next day, unless it was later still. But that doesn't show that it wasn't Tony. He may have come back next evening."

Superintendent Davis did not dispute this somewhat negative analysis. He only said: "Well, it all goes to show how important that diary's likely to be. One of them may come to wish he'd talked about Saturday a bit more, and said less about other days. We can't be too quiet about that. Not till we've got them to talk a bit more than they have yet."

"Yes. It's the best card in the pack for us. The best of a poor lot. But they couldn't well help saying that. Not if the tale was to be that they both saw him. We could have found out easily that they don't come home together on that day. But I can't see that it gets us anywhere, all the same. We've just got one more suspect on the list."

Superintendent Davis was inclined to be more hopeful. Every fresh fact to him was like a further bit of a jigsaw puzzle falling into its place. But he agreed that the suspects were now three. No one could say that Vestman's record made it improbable that he would attempt to rob the flat of a lonely man, or resort to violence if he were discovered in the attempt.

"I suppose you told them that we should want a statement from them?"

"Yes. I told them they'd better both be here at ten-thirty tomorrow morning. Vestman didn't look pleased, and the woman tried some excuse about not leaving the shop, but he interposed at that—I suppose he'd thought better of it—and said they'd be glad to be any help they could, though he was afraid it wouldn't be much."

"Well, we shall be the best ones to judge that when we've got something signed."

The superintendent knew that the statement of a guilty man, after he has been expertly questioned, will usually contain some damaging and probable lies, even where there may be little occasion for him to leave the path of the simpler truth. The trouble is that the statement of an innocent one may prove to be of a very similar character.

CHAPTER XIII.

A QUARREL AT LOVEJOY'S FLAT

THE conversation which followed Mr. Newman's departure might have been illuminating in some particulars, though different from anything he would have expected to hear.

Jane Lovejoy glanced at the clock. "I thought," she said, "he would never go!" She turned alertly towards the couch on which she had thrown her hat and gloves when she came in. "The tea things will have to wait. I want to get out while the shops are open."

Her husband asked: "What's the hurry now?" He no longer maintained the aspect of cheerfulness which he had imperfectly shown to their legal guest. He had the look of a harassed man.

He was debating in a vexed mind whether he should tell her of the sinister hint which Mr. Jellipot had so discreetly given. Would her own discretion increase by being warned of the suspicion which was being directed upon them, or would she lose her head, and say or do foolish things which would make the position worse than it was now?

There had been little of real confidence between these two during the short period of their married life. They had not been divided merely by difference of age. That may be no obstacle to comradeship if the younger partner be of sympathetic intelligence, even in the absence of the love by which all differences will be overcome. But they had, in fact, little in common. She had married a man who had wooed her with some persistence rather than conspicuous ardour, to whom she had been mildly drawn, but mainly influenced by desire to escape from a position of irksome penury, and because marriage was her natural goal. She had expected something better than a bailiff on the kitchen chair!

She liked simple gaieties, in which she had expected to have the means to indulge. But he would, even under more favourable circumstances, have had little inclination for such pursuits. His business would have absorbed most of his time, and more of his thoughts, even had it been prosperous and easy to run. As it was, he had neither leisure, money, nor mood for anything but the bitter struggle which had been forced upon him. He came home for an evening meal and an evening rest, and his conversation—if he would talk at all—would be of the business troubles he had experienced during the day, or anticipated on the next—those, and the petty economies, the petty vexations, which must be contrived or endured by those who have the disease of an empty purse.

She was of a natural amativeness, which, had he been normally responsive, might have maintained a sufficient bond; but as the strain of anxiety and overwork had increased, he had shown, even in this respect, a diminished inclination to give her that which is a wife's due.

A child might have bridged the gap which had been widening between them, and given her an interest in life which would have made her less conscious of other needs, but he had refused her that on the plea of financial stress. Many would say that circumstances had justified him in this decision, but, be that as it may, the price of unnatural living has to be paid.

It was not that they normally quarrelled, though there were sharp words from him at times, to which she would respond with sulky silence or easy tears. Rather, there had been a growing indifference, a lowered temperature of marital intercourse, more ominous than any quarrel could be.

If she had found some consolation in other directions during the long hours when he must leave her alone, she might have said in her own defence that she had given nothing away which he had shown eagerness to retain. And as (so she thought) he had been without suspicion of what she did, it had been almost guiltless satisfaction to her.

When he asked: "What's the hurry now?" there was irritation in his voice. He did not want her to go out. He wanted to talk. A murderer or an innocent though suspected man may equally feel the need of sympathy and support, if he thinks that the police are inclined to charge him with such a crime. Edwin Lovejoy was not one who would often ask sympathy from his fellows. He had a manner which made no friends. Even when he had confided his financial troubles to his own wife, it had been in tones of sarcastic bitterness, rather than in more appealing or weaker moods.

"I want," she said, "to buy lots of things. Shoes, for one. There won't be much time tonight, but I want to do what I can."

But he did not want her to go out, for whatever purpose, urgent or not. He wanted to talk to her in a way that he seldom did. And besides—"lots of things?" The money hadn't been meant for that. She seemed to him callous, abrupt, thinking only to take instant advantage for herself, regardless of him.

This was only partly fair, for she could not be expected to sympathize with a worry of which she had not been told, but feelings are often illogical, and yet may be instinctively sound.

"There can't be such a hurry as that. You can get shoes tomorrow."

The words, perhaps the tone, brought a look of obstinacy to her face. "I'd rather get them tonight. Just look at these! You haven't cared much how I've been dressed. I've not been fit to go out anywhere. After all, it's my money."

The remark may have been regretted when it was said, as quickly spoken words often are. But spoken words are hard to unsay, especially when they are true. They gave Edwin Lovejoy an unpleasant intimation of the new relationship which Adrian Rissole's money might establish between them. Hitherto, she had been financially dependent upon him. He might not have provided for her as liberally as she had expected, or as he would have liked to do, but everything she had had, such as it was, she had—or so he supposed—owed to him. Now she was about to become personally independent. Worse than that, the position threatened that he might become financially dependent upon her. He attributed her last remark to a clearer perception of this than, in fact, she had; and resentment might have made him silent had he not seen a fallacy in her argument which could be used in effectual retort.

"It's not your money for spending just as you like. It's been found for special purposes on our joint names. If you've got the decency to wait a few weeks—I don't suppose it will be more than that—you can spend Adrian's money any way you like and just let the business smash."

"You know I didn't mean that! It wouldn't be much to buy one pair of shoes out of what we've got. And I thought I'd pay Radley's account, and get some poultry for tomorrow. I was only thinking of you."

Self-pity at this partial truth—for it was a fact that Edwin did like poultry, which an unpaid bill had rendered it hazardous to order during recent weeks—and realization that while they argued the time went, brought an outbreak of facile tears.

Her husband looked at her gloomily. He made no motion to comfort her, but a note of apology had come into the irritation of his voice as he answered: "Well, you needn't take it like that. You'll get shoes enough before long. You can get a pair tomorrow. I dare say I could pay for them. But that lawyer Jellipot hinted at another trouble today, and I was wanting to tell you about that. I don't want to worry you, but I think it's something you ought to know. He seemed to think that the police might try to make out that I killed Adrian about as likely as not."

For a long moment his wife made no answer. She looked at him with frightened, astonished eyes in a whitening face. "They'll say you killed Adrian?" she repeated. "But why should they say that?"

She made no further motion to go out. She pulled off the threadbare gloves which she had been drawing on a moment before. She sat down at a distance from him.

He looked at her curiously, as though being as much interested in the way she took it as in that which he had to tell. She repeated stupidly: "But why should they say that?"

"Because we needed the money. And because no one had a better opportunity. That's quite easy to see."

"But that doesn't say you did! They might say anyone did it, if they argue backwards like that. It's their business to find out the truth, and not frighten people by inventing things that they can't prove. It would be horrible if they started such talk as that."

There was genuine-sounding indignation in her voice, but there was noticeable relief also, as though the reason he gave had not been that which she had expected and feared to hear.

If he were conscious of this, he passed it without remark, answering her argument in a sober way.

"I don't suppose they'll start any talk. It wouldn't be the police way. I only hope they won't try anything worse. But there can't be anything they can prove, and I don't see what we should have to fear without that.

"It was that lawyer Jellipot who put the idea into my head. There's some legal point that the money wouldn't come to us if we'd killed Adrian to get it. Mr. Jellipot seemed to take it quite seriously at first, though he must have felt differently afterwards, or he wouldn't have helped us the way he did."

"Then there can't be much cause to worry."

"Perhaps not. But it's only sense to go over what happened, and see if there's any way they could put it on to me."

"They can't possibly do that. I should have thought it would be more sense to mind our own affairs, and take no notice at all."

"So it might. But it's natural to talk it over between ourselves."

"I don't see what there is to say, except that it's just absurd."

"They haven't found any weapon yet. We'd have to decide what to say if they wanted to come here searching for that."

"We'd let them search, of course. What else could we do? I don't suppose we could stop them, if we were silly enough to try. They'd get tired before they found anything here."

But as she said this, a look of fear came over her face. "There's the kitchen knife I cut up the rabbit with yesterday. I dare say they'd find some blood on that."

"Since yesterday? I dare say they would! But I believe they could tell rabbit's blood from that of a man."

Jane understood the sarcasm of her husband's exclamation. She knew that her housekeeping tidiness fell short of his exacting standards. She said weakly: "Well, there are so many knives!" So there were. Perhaps it was not surprising in an ironmonger's house.

But to rely upon anyone being able to distinguish accurately between the stains of rabbits' or human blood did not sound very safe to her. She said: "Anyway, I'd better give it a good wash. And while I'm about it, I'd better go over the lot, and make sure." Suddenly her face whitened as it had not done even when he startled her by his first remark. *Was that what he had meant her to do?* Her voice rose shrilly as she exclaimed: "Edwin, you didn't really do it yourself, did you? You don't mean that the knife's here?"

Edwin Lovejoy looked at his wife with a cold anger which, for a moment, appeared to obstruct his speech. Or was he debating what would be wisest to say? What would be the most natural reaction of an innocent man to such a suggestion from his wife's lips? Had Mr. Newman been able to listen to this conversation, he might have concluded that Jane was an innocent woman both in act and knowledge, but of her husband he would have formed a less certain opinion.

Now he said, after that moment's pause: "Of course I didn't! You know that perfectly well. It was you who started all this talk about washing knives. I don't care if you've got rabbits' blood on every one in the kitchen drawer. I didn't kill him; and what motive could I have had? I didn't even know that he'd made a will. I didn't take it to be more than talk about leaving something to you. Lots of men talk like that, and never pick up a pen."

"I'm sorry, Edwin. Of course, I didn't mean it. I just feel frightened. I know you wouldn't have done anything like that. You'd have had no motive at all. I've got all worked up. I wish he hadn't left the money to me. I told him—"

She stopped abruptly.

The sudden pause, the look of a new fear, that passed like a shadow across her face, gave an added significance to the interrupted exclamation.

"What did you tell Adrian?" he asked sharply.

"Nothing. I hardly know what I'm saying. I'm not used to such things as this."

"I believe you know something you won't say."

"How could I? You know I didn't know anything. You know how anxious I was to find out why we didn't see him."

"Then tell me what you told him that you're afraid to say now."

"I'm not afraid. It was just nothing that matters. It can't matter now. He said he'd lend us some money if we were hard up, and I told him we'd rather not."

"Why did you tell him that?"

"Because—well, because I knew it would all be no good. I knew he'd never see it again."

"What do you mean by that?"

"I could tell that from the way you talked."

"You seem to have thought of his interests more than mine."

"More than ours you might say. You don't suppose I *like* nothing ever being paid when it's due? I just wanted to keep as straight as I could."

Edwin listened to an explanation in which he could not entirely believe. He felt that there was lack of candour here, though he was unsure what it might mean. He asked: "How did he know we were hard up?"

"He said he could hear us when we talked louder than usual. He said it was wonderful how the sound would sometimes carry down into his room. "

"And you never told me of this? You didn't care how we gave ourselves away?"

"I didn't think much about it. We hadn't got to talk loud. I shouldn't say that we often do. And he only mentioned it just before—before the last time he came up to see us. And I didn't know it was true. I don't now. He might have just made it up to explain something he'd found out in another way."

"You never heard sounds going down to his room?"

"No, how could we? This room was always empty when we were there."

Mr. Lovejoy saw reason in that. It had been a silly question to ask. He wondered whether sounds would come up in the same way. He'd never heard any. But Adrian Rissole had been a lonely man. He wouldn't talk to himself. And perhaps they wouldn't. He knew little about acoustics, but he had understood that they were unaccountably queer. But there was something wrong somewhere. A lack of frankness, if not a lie. He did not believe that she would have refused money for such a reason, and have said nothing to him about the offer having been made. Not with her home threatened the way it had been. He thought that no woman would.

He changed the subject to ask: "You knew that he'd made the will?"

She looked confused again. "I knew what he'd said about it. So did you. He could do that if he liked. It couldn't matter what became of the money when he was dead."

"Well, he's dead now. There's no doubt of that." The tone in which this was said implied that there was little else that was sure in a world of doubt. As he said it, Edwin Lovejoy got up. He said he would take a walk. He wanted to think things over. Jane made no protest. She had forgotten both Radley's account and those dreadful heels. Had Chief Inspector Combridge looked in half an hour later, he would have been interested to find her surrounded by three or four knives of various sizes, giving them the best clean they had ever had.

She thought that she knew who had killed Adrian. She had thought she knew all along. She was almost sure still. She had not thought of it being Edwin before tonight. She still did not think it was he. She was *almost* sure it was not. Almost, but not quite. And it was a dreadful doubt.

CHAPTER XIV.

THE MISSES RANGER WERE SHOCKED

CHIEF INSPECTOR COMBRIDGE spent the next three days in the patient pursuit of usually irrelevant facts which is the prosaic foundation upon which every charge relying upon circumstantial evidence must be built.

He took statements from Mr. and Mrs. Aide, which, after some hours of probing questions, and apparently candid answers, contained little of value he had not already learned. They professed to know nothing they had not voluntarily told at his first interview with them. They had not cultivated the acquaintance of neighbours. As to those on the upper floors of Barclay Buildings, they had never even ascended their stairs. They could not have said with certainty on which floors they lived. Their knowledge of them was confined to occasional passings as they went in or out; their acquaintance to the bare formality of recognition which such contacts require. It began and ended at that.

Having taken these statements, he proceeded to investigation of their business activities, and discovered nothing to increase a suspicion which, as yet, had no foundation beyond the known characters of the couple, and the opportunity which had been theirs. He found that their Dean Street business, which they had purchased for £1,300 on returning to England, was genuine, conducted with average honesty, and mildly prosperous. It had not attracted the unfavourable notice of the police of the Soho district, as it certainly would had it become a resort of any criminal associates. This was no more than negative evidence, but it supported their contention that they had come back to their own country with the intention of living law-respecting and respectable lives. If that were so (which his experiences did not render it easy to believe), few things could have happened which would be more unwelcome than a murder in their own vicinity.

Vestman, being interviewed a third time, and in a somewhat more courteous manner than had been shown to him at the first, professed his disposition to assist in the discovery of the criminal by any means in his power. What did the police wish him to do?

He was told that he could do nothing but keep open eyes for the possibility of encountering the seaman whom he could identify as Adrian Rissole's acquaintance. Obviously, if this man were the murderer, it was a poor hope. But if he were innocent of the crime, what was more likely than that, having frequently called before, he would. do so again?

Vestman's offer, if he were innocent himself, might be honestly meant. He could not fail to see that suspicion would never wholly remove from his own door while the culprit should not be known. But there appeared to be little useful that he could tell, or that he would be likely to do.

An enquiry concerning the late tenants of the first floor flat disclosed that they had left less than six weeks before the probable date of the murder—two elderly maiden ladies, neither of whom was likely to be concerned in such a crime, nor able to throw any light upon it. But Inspector Combridge did not omit to interview them also.

He found them in a Surbiton flat: the Misses Ranger. Milly, a thin tall austere lady, was deaf. Kitty, shorter, equally thin, but not equally austere, was spokeswoman for both. She appeared afraid to say things which her elder sister, though declining to sustain the conversation herself, insisted should be disclosed.

Milly, when she did speak, produced sentences of extreme grammatical accuracy. Kitty was colloquial to the verge of illiteracy. "Though I didn't ought to say that," was her frequent phrase.

By the exercise of sufficient patience, and his pleasantest manner, he heard much, and learned something which might be remotely helpful—at least, on the supposition that it was the hand of Edwin Lovejoy which had struck the blow. It was scarcely evidence bearing on the crime, but might be a pointer showing in which direction such evidence should be sought.

The ladies had (of course) read of the murder, and congratulated themselves on the discretion which had inclined them to move before it occurred.

They did not actually imply that they had anticipated the event, but they inferred that it was consistent with the general atmosphere of the upper floors of Barclay Buildings. "Tell the officer," Milly directed her sister, "of the unseemly incidents of which we were compelled to be cognisant."

Kitty, with some coyness, narrated the "unseemly incidents"—"goings-on" as she preferred to describe them—which had disturbed their maidenly peace.

Of the Aides they had no complaint: quiet respectable married people who were out all day, kept themselves to themselves, and showed neighbourly civility when occasions of contact came. But those on the upper floors! It was not only that the Lovejoys did not pay their bills, were known to have had their credit stopped by successive butchers, believed to take in summonses as regularly as more reputable people take in the *Daily Express*, and suspected of having had bailiffs upon their premises upon one occasion, if not more—this might have been endured, although the contamination had been very close, and irregularity in settlement of accounts was regarded by these ladies of untempted rectitude as a deliberate perversity, impossible to people of honest minds. Of an even more sinister complexion had been the relations of Mrs. Lovejoy and the third-floor tenant. The acoustic peculiarity observed by Adrian Rissole appeared to be a repeated feature of the architecture of Barclay Buildings. The ladies—or, at least, Kitty, who was not afflicted by deafness—had heard conversations indicative of depths of moral depravity, such as maiden ladies can only hint in the vaguest terms.

But the vaguest terms may be rendered forcible by grimace and gesture, supported by suggestion of understatement. Kitty made it plain that, though she might not have seen much, she had heard unspeakable things. She contrived to suggest Mrs. Lovejoy in the part of a trusted wife who betrays her husband during the hours that he labours for her support, and, at the same time, as being married to a man who basely (though not very successfully, as it appeared) lived in shameless partnership on her immoral earnings. Was it wonderful that any people who valued their own reputations should prefer to remove from premises of such dubious respectability?

Inspector Combridge was too experienced in the appraisement of such testimony not to recognize an almost certain basis of fact. Excess of imagination there might be; but it was not a reasonable supposition that these women would have left Barclay Buildings—whether reasonably or not—on such a pretext, had there been no ground whatever for the allegations which he now heard. And he knew the assertion of Lovejoy's financial exigencies to be no more than the truth. That concerning Mrs. Lovejoy's illicit relations with the dead man was not so clearly confirmed—might, indeed, be said to be discounted by the fact that Adrian Rissole had been on friendly terms with husband as well as wife, and that, if Jane Lovejoy had visited him during the daytime, it might have been with her husband's knowledge and ready consent. Some basis of fact was here also, but how much had imagination added thereto?

The question might become important. It suggested jealousy as an alternative, or perhaps supplementary, motive to that of greed. Slightly, it increased the probability that Lovejoy was the guilty man. There might come a time when a subpœna would oblige Kitty to tell her tale in *Rex v. Lovejoy* with greater particularity than she had now felt it seemly to do. But, for the moment, he decided not even to ask her for one of the signed statements which are of the routine of such investigations.

The case against Edwin Lovejoy must be considered with the knowledge that this evidence was in reserve. If it should appear to be of the minimum strength which justifies an arrest, he would see Kitty again. He thought that he would not only bring her to the point of more explicit disclosure of what she had overheard, but to a more reliable standard of exactitude, if she knew that she would be required to give evidence in a public court. And he was not as yet endeavouring to build up a case against Edwin Lovejoy. He was merely seeking the truth, which might be the more difficult quest, and aiming to do so with an open mind. When he had reached a settled opinion, he might—however unconsciously—approach such a question rather differently.

The importance of avoiding any premature conclusion was demonstrated when he returned to Scotland Yard from his Surbiton visit, and found that a cable had come in from the New York police. It read:

> Tony Rissole signed on, Manhattan New York February 5th paid off Southampton February 11th stop cannot trace return here stop previously 88 East 27th Street stop no communication with that address since February 5th though effects still there stop enquiries continuing stop.

The effect of this cable was that the question of the arrest of Edwin Lovejoy, to which the Assistant Commissioner had previously been disposed, was deferred, while enquiries were actively pursued either to establish that Tony Rissole had returned to America, or to locate him in this country.

As the matter now stood, while there was no direct evidence connecting him with the crime, apart from the assertion of the other suspect that he had met one such as he on the stairs of Barclay Buildings on the Friday evening of, or before, the crime—the significance of which was reduced by the witness of the diary that the murder could hardly have been committed before the evening of the next day—yet it was now established that he had arrived in Europe a few days earlier, and the fact that he had not since appeared at, or communicated with, his New York lodging was at least consistent with the probable action of a man having blood on his hands, and in terror of the pursuit of the outraged law.

With the case against Lovejoy no stronger than it was, it became an elementary precaution to eliminate Tony Rissole before proceeding upon it, especially as there was no probability that anything would be lost by that delay. For it was extremely unlikely that Edwin Lovejoy would attempt flight; and even that possibility would not be considered disadvantageous by the police, for it might be no less than a decisive addition to the weight of circumstantial evidence on which a conviction must be obtained. And it was certain that he would not get far away: he was too closely shadowed for that.

It was at this stage that Inspector Combridge decided that it might be profitable to give Mr. Jellipot another call. He was not unmindful of the policy of reticence which Superintendent Davis had impressed upon him. But he thought to obtain information, rather than to impart it. He was still curious to learn why the solicitor's clerk should have had occasion to visit Barclay Buildings. When he knew that, he might better decide how much could be told on his side.

Past experience caused him to be wary of proceeding against anyone whom Mr. Jellipot might elect to defend, but the dead man had been the solicitor's own client. Considering that fact, and the circumstances of the crime, he came to a sound conviction that Mr. Jellipot would not be disposed to defend anyone who might be charged with it, unless he were very sure that he would be exerting himself on behalf of an innocent man.

CHAPTER XV.

THE OPINION OF MR. JELLIPOT

MR. JELLIPOT received Inspector Combridge with his usual quiet cordiality. If he were busily occupied—and it was seldom that this was not the case—he did not allow the interview to be shortened by the contending claims of the business day. He telephoned to his outer office that he was not to be disturbed unless by a matter of particular urgency. He laid down the instrument to say: "I have been expecting that you would look in."

"Well, I thought you might like to know how our enquiries are getting on. And I shall be rather interested to hear what you made of the ironmonger and his wife."

"I have formed no settled opinion," Mr. Jellipot answered cautiously. "I should be grateful for any additional information you can give me which might assist towards a clearer one than I now have."

Chief Inspector Combridge hesitated. He had great respect for any opinion which the solicitor might express. It might be foolish not to tell him all that he knew, if he were to be rewarded by so valuable a judgment thereon. But past experience of one case—indeed, more than one—which had developed in unexpected, and, for him, unsatisfactory directions, made him cautious now.

He said bluntly: "I should like to know first that you won't be acting for Lovejoy, if I get instructions to run him in."

Mr. Jellipot answered with unusual energy: "I'm not acting for anyone in this matter, nor intending to do so." A common memory, and a habitual caution, caused him to add: "When I say that, it is, of course, not to be taken as a promise. It is statement of future intention and present fact, which it is most improbable that I should see reason to change."

After another moment of silence, he continued: "You need not doubt that I am as anxious as you can be that the murderer of Adrian

Rissole should be correctly identified. He would certainly have no help from me."

"Yes. I felt sure you would feel like that. The fact is that we're not sure. There's a lot of cause for suspicion against Lovejoy, and some of us are inclined to think that it goes further than that. But we've just heard from New York that Tony landed at Southampton on February 11th, and he's 'gone, no address' since then, which looks bad. We've got to thank you for putting us on his trail. And there's another man we should look on as a likely candidate for the dock, if there weren't these two already with better claims."

Mr. Jellipot's interest obviously quickened at this announcement. "Then it sounds," he said, "as though it may be a more interesting problem than first appeared. Perhaps you would tell me first how the third man comes on the scene."

It was a question which even Superintendent Davis might not have hesitated to answer without reserve. Mr. Aide (alias Vestman) was most unlikely to be numbered among Mr. Jellipot's clients, nor was it reasonable to suppose that any circumstances would arise under which the solicitor would undertake his defence, if his prosecution should follow. He told all that he knew.

Mr. Jellipot listened intently, but when he spoke it was evident that he was not greatly impressed.

"You have," he said, "as I see it, nothing against Vestman except his past record, concerning which you may say that your experience leads you to attach a more ominous value than a mere layman in the science of crime detection—such as myself—would be likely to do.

"We have a man who is strongly suspected—you might put it more highly than that—of having been associated in the commission of a number of burglaries with a brother who has been hanged for homicidal violence when interrupted in such a crime. You believe this man to have been present on that occasion, so that, in law at least, he was equally guilty. In fact, it is a fifty-fifty chance that he may have been the actual murderer.

"This is certainly bad, even allowing for the fact that he appears to have gone straight subsequently, and that your enquiries have not disclosed that he is at present associating with criminal circles—"

"But that," Inspector Combridge interrupted, "is something they never did. The Vestmans always kept to themselves. That was why they were so hard to follow."

"Then we may eliminate that qualification, and say simply that his record is bad, and the crime was such a one as he might commit.

But before we go on to conclude that he actually did so, we must observe that there are some important arguments on the other side.

"You have a man who had narrowly escaped prosecution on a capital charge, and who may have deserved—or else the basis of your suspicion against him goes—the penalty from which a false alibi so barely saved him. Since then, he has successfully—cunningly, if you will—avoided the observation of the police. He has a business which, if your information regarding it be reliable, frees him from any acute anxiety either as to his present or future comfort. Such a man has much more to lose than to gain if he deliberately returns to his old pursuits.

"But if he should do so—and I can see that you are about to tell me that when criminal instincts are in the blood they may dominate reasonable considerations—would he have attempted robbery so close to his own dwelling, where it was essential to his long-established secrecy that the police should not enquire? The fox—so I have read—will not rob the hen roost that is near to its own earth.

"Beyond that, you have to consider the circumstances of the murder. The others in which Vestman is thought to have been involved were acts of panic to silence those who, had they been allowed to live, might have detained, or subsequently denounced, the criminals. But Adrian Rissole was stabbed in the back, under circumstances which suggest that he was unsuspicious of his visitor or of impending violence. He was stabbed either by a man of whose presence he did not know, or one to whom he had opened a willing door.

"As to that, you will say that Vestman was known to him. He would have let him enter without suspicion. So he might. But if Vestman stabbed him at the next moment, it must have been a premeditated course of action, by a man who must have known that, even if he should escape immediate detection, subsequent enquiry must bring the police to his door. Even though he might not be charged with the crime, there would be much which he had been patient to gain which he would almost certainly lose—as in fact he has. Perhaps even more if he were resuming criminal courses than if he were continuing to pursue an honest life. It has, to me, a most improbable sound.

"And there is a further point. You tell me that Vestman did not merely deny knowledge of the crime, as he would be certain to do. He asserted that he had never ascended the stairs to the upper floors. That is, of course, no more than the word of a man whose veracity is particularly unreliable, and as such we may be tempted to put it too lightly aside. For is it likely, if it were not true, that he would make so needless an assertion, which eyewitnesses might confute, with the result of augmenting suspicion against himself by the weight of a superfluous lie? In the absence of such controverting evidence, I should be disposed to accept his word."

Inspector Combridge listened to this rather prolix, but very lucid analysis, and though he thought that—fortunately for his department—the average British criminal did not act upon such carefully balanced reasoning as Mr. Jellipot was in the habit of applying to the problems that engaged his mind, he saw no reason to doubt the soundness of the conclusions to which it had now led.

"That," he said, "sounds reasonable enough. I'd better tell you next what we've learned about Tony Rissole, and I shall be glad if you can put him in his place in the same way. I've told you that he landed at Southampton on the eleventh of last month, and hasn't been heard of since. As far as we can make out, he hasn't gone back to America, and we can't find him here, though we've done everything possible, and it's the kind of thing at which we don't often fail."

"Yes," Mr. Jellipot agreed, "I have noticed that. As a matter of fact I have observed the description you have circulated, though I am not a very regular reader of the daily press. I may tell you that the photograph which you have distributed is more accurate than such reproductions usually are. I recognized the man before I read the caption beneath the picture. "

"Well, that's a bull point for us. But we can't find him, and I don't know that we could do more than question him if we did. It's not a crime to stay here, and he might have a dozen excuses ready. As a matter of fact, I believe he's a London man. But if you'll tell me what you think—I mean whether he's the man it's our business to catch—I'll be glad to listen."

"There is a proverb," Mr. Jellipot smiled in reply, "about making bricks without straw. Even the Israelites—a people more patient and industrious than I am ever likely to be—did not find it an easy task; and it is one which I shall not attempt to achieve. I have little doubt that either the New York police, or your equally efficient Metropolitan organization, will trace the man before many weeks have passed, and we may then hope that we shall have more data on which to judge."

"I hope you're right about that! But there's still the case against Lovejoy, and if he's the culprit we're wasting time over these other men. You know as much as I do about him, and perhaps a bit more, and—" Inspector Combridge checked himself with the realization that his words somewhat outran the truth while he omitted to mention the diary of the dead man—and yet how, if at all, could that be material to the question of Lovejoy's innocence or guilt? It was with a perverted instinct of frankness, where the occasion for reticence really did not exist, that he ended this sudden pause by saying: "I'll tell you what's on my mind. I don't like not to be frank. We've known each other too long for that. The fact is I saw Newman come out of Barclay's Buildings. I couldn't help wondering why he was there, and whether it meant that you were working up the Lovejoys' defence, ready to give us a toss if we ran him in."

"The interpretation was perhaps natural," Mr. Jellipot conceded, his mind dwelling the while in admiration upon the ubiquity of the C.I.D., "but I can assure you that it was entirely wrong. My clerk was there with no further object than to pay out an execution which had been levied upon the effects of the Lovejoys' flat."

He gave this answer as though supplying all the information necessary to convince the inspector of the error of his previous deduction, but it is not surprising that it was taken differently.

"If you're lending him money, you must be feeling it's a sure thing that Rissole wasn't killed with his ironmongery!"

"As a matter of fact, I am not lending him money. Not directly, that is. I did no more than to give him an introduction to a respectable bank, where an advance could be obtained upon the joint names of himself and his wife, in view of Mrs. Lovejoy's expectations under the will which it is my business to prove."

He paused, and then added, as he watched the face of a man from whom the cloud of doubt had not entirely lifted: "To be exact, I should add that I guaranteed the bank, which in my position as executor for Adrian Rissole, and in my judgment of what his wishes would be, I considered it to be my duty to do."

"Well, that comes to the same thing. Rissole couldn't have wanted you to help a man who'd stuck a knife in his back."

"Probably not. But the question was less simple than that. It is Jane Lovejoy to whom the money is left, and whom my late client desired to benefit. Adrian Rissole—I may have told you before?—was a man of habitual procrastination, and the fact that he did not merely intend, but actually exerted himself to execute this will, shows a much stronger impulse than would necessarily be indicated in one of different temperament. Indeed, he told me that had he not—but I feel I am prolix in explanation, as it is my weakness to be."

The solicitor checked himself, in entire unconsciousness that he had been on the verge of saying something which might have had a material effect upon the course of the events that followed. He added: "But I must still give you a word of further explanation. So contrary is the truth from the theory which you have been disposed to adopt that it is extremely improbable that I should have given this guarantee had I been convinced that I was talking to an innocent man.

"Indeed, the question would not have arisen, for I should have felt able to give his own solicitors the assurance which they required from me before granting him accommodation of which he was, as you know, in acute need. It was the fact that, as a matter of professional honour, I felt unable to give that assurance, which led me—as I reflected upon the serious consequences to himself which that scrupulosity would entail, and which threatened at least equal distress to his wife for whom my client had wished to provide—to decide upon a course which would free me from regret or self-reproach under whatever development there might be.

"If Edwin Lovejoy be innocent, I shall always be free from the vexatious thought that I had injured him through a groundless doubt. If he be guilty, I shall have lost a sum which I can afford to spare."

"Yes. I see what you mean. But I shouldn't say there are many lawyers who'd have looked at it in the same way."

Mr. Jellipot looked embarrassed, even distressed, at this comment. "There are," he said, "doubtless many members of my profession—men of moderate incomes, and family obligations which are not mine—who could not honourably or prudently take such a risk, however strongly disposed they might be. But, in my case, it was a selfishness which I could indulge."

He turned the subject next moment by adding: "But a question came to me as we talked, which you will doubtless be able to answer.

"I was debating the possibility of Tony Rissole having returned to his own—or rather his adopted—country in a way that you would be unable to trace, which appeared to me to be difficult, if not impossible, in view of the papers of identification which are required, both when boarding a vessel on this side and when landing there, and assuming that, had he signed on as a member of any crew, the record would be easy to find. And as I puzzled over this question, I was led to recall that you have told me that Vestman and his female companion had returned here, under another name, and in such a way as to avoid the observation of the police, and I wondered how it could be done."

"There's no mystery about that," Inspector Combridge answered readily "and not much trouble to such as they. It's a matter of knowing where to get what you want, and not minding the risk of being spotted by an observation officer who's known you before in your right name. There must be hundreds, if not thousands, who get through that way every year, for one who gets caught. It's just a matter of buying a suitable passport, stolen, traded, or faked. The faked ones are the most dangerous to use.

"You needn't suppose that Vestman first took the name of Aide, and then got hold of a passport to correspond. That might have been difficult. But he'd have a choice among hundreds, pick the most suitable—the photograph has to be moderately alike—and then take whatever name was on it.

"When you think how many people there are who never go abroad, and that any of them can get a passport for about eight-and-sixpence, and sell it for five pounds, if they know where to go, you can be sure there's a brisk trade. It's just a matter of supply and demand. "

"But in the case of 'Mr. and Mrs. Aide'—I should have supposed that *two* photographs on the same passport—"

"Yes, of course. But she probably travelled separately, as a spinster or widow, in another name. Besides that, photographs can be changed, and we know that they often are."

"I have always regarded the passport nuisance," Mr. Jellipot replied seriously, "as one of the worst products of the last war. I had understood that the one valid argument in its defence—and a very poor one, since no man can be in two places at the same time, and every transit must be equivalent loss and gain—was that it rendered it difficult for criminals or agitators to move from one country to another. But you tell me that it is ineffectual, even for that."

"Oh, I wouldn't say it's no good at all!" Inspector Combridge answered, rising to go as he spoke. "But it's a racket. I'll give you that."

Mr. Jellipot showed no disposition to pursue the subject further. He shook hands with cordiality, following his visitor to the door. He had some thoughts of vested interests and bureaucratic tyrannies which he did not speak, knowing that they would be received with no more than perfunctory interest. The inspector would have said that that was because he was a practical man.

78

CHAPTER XVI.

THE TRAILING OF TONY RISSOLE

THE operation of tracing the movements of Tony Rissole proceeded with the normal thoroughness of the police in such matters, and, up to a point, with normal celerity and normal success.

A comprehensive enquiry among Southampton lodging houses frequented by seafaring men disclosed two addresses at either of which he would put up at times. At one of these he was in debt to his landlady for a considerable sum borrowed some years before on representations which had caused her to complain to the police when it was not returned, and had come near to acquainting him with the inside of an English prison. He had, however, prevailed upon her not to proceed against him, and from time to time had made some reductions in the amount of his debt.

It appeared probable that he put up with her while at Southampton when he arrived with the intention of making such a payment, but otherwise at a Northam address about two miles away.

On landing on February 11th, he had gone to this woman, a Mrs. Trufitt, and had stayed till Wednesday, the 18th inst, when he had left, taking his luggage with him, but saying that he would return, after going up to London for a few days, when he would make a payment both to cover the accommodation he had received and to reduce his earlier indebtedness.

Mrs. Trufitt had agreed with protest, as there had been a similar incident during the previous year, when his promise had been fulfilled, but this time he had neither come nor communicated further.

Other enquiries concerning the missing man had exposed him as having the reputation of one whom quiet peace-loving men would not be anxious to meet. A ship's carpenter may be a less important individual than was the case before the discovery that it is possible to cross the seas in a metal pot, but his occupation is still respectable, and carpenters, both by land and sea, are proverbially men to trust. But Tony Rissole was said to be both violent and cunning. It was a particularly damning fact that he had stabbed a man during a drunken quarrel in the "Roper's Arms" three years before, and was considered fortunate to have been let off with a £10 fine, on the plea that a prison sentence would cause him to lose his ship, and might make it difficult for him to re-enter the United States, he not being a citizen of that country—a land which is particularly inhospitable to alien criminals, having quite enough of its own. Tony's ancestry might be predominantly Italian, but the discredit of his birth belonged to a Hoxton slum.

There was abundant evidence of his movements and occupations until the Wednesday when he had stated that he was leaving for London, but at that point it entirely ceased. It was exhaustively proved that he had not signed again on any ocean liner, either from Southampton, London, or any other British port. The smaller tramp steamers would not be likely to take on one of his specialized qualifications, nor would he be likely to seek such a berth unless he were endeavouring to hide his movements, but this possibility was not ignored. Even that he might have sailed as a passenger was considered, and examined with much negative industry.

With the assistance of the press and the B.B.C., his description was circulated throughout the country. The police, it was said, desired to interview him in connection with the Rissole murder. Public assistance was requested to enable them to trace him. A recent photograph, supplied by Mrs. Trufitt, was widely published.

While these enquiries proceeded, a letter reached Scotland Yard from the New York police, with an enclosure which increased Superintendent Davis's desire to have a talk with the missing man.

Even when the public purse is available on which to draw (and the British public is officially supposed to be so desperately anxious that any man suspected of murder should be caught that it is utterly indifferent to the amount of its money which may be disbursed for so great a purpose), letters will still tend to be more informative than a cabled message.

The enclosure was a sheet of notepaper, somewhat soiled, but with its pencilled record clearly decipherable, which the New York police, with a disregard of the niceties of legal right more characteristic of their own than of English methods, had abstracted from the belongings which the missing man had left in his abandoned Twenty-Seventh Street lodgings.

It appeared to be the undated draft of a letter, which had been kept for reference. It had alterations and erasures, but read substantially thus:

Dear Adrian,

I am coming to London next month, and sending this in advance, so that you'll get some time to chew on it. I only want what's fair, but I'm not going to be put off longer till you check out and all the bucks go to that pert young bitch on the floor above. I've seen too much not to know what it's likely to be, if I don't cash in now.

Give me my whack, and you can go to hell your own way with no more trouble from me, but I won't stand for being put off again. So get ready for a share-out when I knock at the door, and if you don't die of old age it won't be my doing.

Your affectionate cousin,

Tony

The first effect of this document was to turn the suspicions of the police more strongly upon its author, and to remove their shadow from Edwin Lovejoy to a corresponding degree.

The letter was both demand and threat, and, if that demand had been presented in person, it had certainly not been granted.

Logical deductions went further than that, for, after writing such a letter, was it not certain that Tony would have called upon his cousin? Did not Mrs. Trufitt's evidence confirm this intention, adding that he had left for London a few days before the probable day of the murder, and mentioning his expectation of obtaining money while there? And if he had called after the crime had been committed, and knocked at a closed door, would he not have made enquiries concerning his cousin's movements, rather than have disappeared from all his accustomed haunts?

The draft letter increased the already strong suspicion against him to a damning degree, but its legal value was of a less certain kind.

First, there was no proof of such a letter having been sent. If it had, it had disappeared; for every document in the dead man's flat had already been subjected to the scrutiny of the police. That was not surprising, for Adrian might have destroyed a letter which must have caused him some annoyance when he received it, especially if he did not consider yielding to its demand. Also, and most probably if it had been kept, it might have been removed by the murderer's hand when he ransacked the box under the bed.

"You can't," Superintendent Davis said, in his sleepier ruminating manner, "call it a blackmailing letter."

Chief Inspector Combridge stared in a momentary astonishment at this verdict. "Can't you?" he retorted. "I should call it one of the nastiest blackmailing letters I ever read."

"Well, so it is," the Superintendent conceded, with the inconsistency which is so often the friend of truth. "But you'll notice it doesn't ask for anything that the writer doesn't profess to believe is really due to himself. An angry man whose money was being fraudulently withheld by a dishonest relative, and spent on vicious women, might write such a letter, and you wouldn't get one jury in twenty to think he'd done anything very wrong.

"If he'd threatened that he'd tell the woman's husband unless he were paid not to, that would be a more serious matter; as it is, it's the last sentence that is the worst, and even that could be twisted by a clever counsel to mean a lot less than it was probably meant to do. And there's a wide difference between the threat by an angry man which is just meant to frighten someone into paying up, and putting a knife into his back."

"Yes—but when the knife's put there a few weeks afterwards!"

"Of course that alters it. I'm not saying it's not a big weight in the scale. I think Tony's the man we want. If there weren't almost equal grounds for suspicion against Lovejoy, I should call it a clear case.

"But I was looking for legal proof, and it seems to me that we should still want a bit more. If we'd got the letter itself, or even evidence that it was ever sent!"

"Well, I say he's the man, and if the case isn't quite all we could wish, he'll probably tell enough lies when we catch him, or when he gets into the box, to put the rope in the right place."

"I expect he will. But there's just one possibility that we oughtn't to overlook. Suppose Tony knocked at Adrian's door, and got no reply, and decided that his cousin had bolted to avoid seeing him, and thought he could make a good guess at where he could have gone—perhaps somewhere a long distance away—and went straight off after him? There'd be no crime in that, even if he did owe something at the rooms he'd left."

It was a possibility which Inspector Combridge was obliged, however reluctantly, to admit. It might have been a more extreme improbability, in view of the fact the man had been murdered by someone, if there were not another candidate with a strong separate claim upon the condemned cell.

"The trouble with this case," he said, "is that whenever we get a bit more evidence against one, we get the next bit against the other. I shall soon be thinking that they both did it, and propose that we arrest the two."

"Well, that's not impossible. Lovejoy might have lent him the knife," the superintendent suggested, with a seriousness of tone which did not deceive his colleague.

"You think," he said, "I'm mucking this up, but I can't see where we've gone wrong. The trouble's with the facts themselves."

"I think you've done as well as you always do—and I think Tony's your man."

Chief Inspector Combridge went off, satisfied with this assurance, which might have sounded more ambiguous to a subtler mind than it was actually meant to be.

Superintendent Davis picked up the pencilled draft again for a closer study. He considered the more legible of the alterations which had been made. They did not help him. The first draft had been milder than the form of words finally chosen. There was nothing of decisive importance in that, but he saw that it could be argued that these alterations implied that the letter had been deliberately composed to frighten, rather than expressing the serious intention of a ruthless man. Only in one particular had it been modified to a milder tone. That was the allusion to the "pert young bitch," who had first been defined by a much coarser adjective. Superintendent Davis concluded that Tony Rissole had not liked Jane Lovejoy, to whom he could not doubt that the description was meant to apply. What had he known—what had he seen—of her?

Here, at last, was evidence strongly confirmatory to that of the Misses Ranger, that there had been some levity of conduct, if not actual marital unfaithfulness, on the part of Jane Lovejoy during her husband's absence; but was not that cause for added suspicion against Edwin Lovejoy even more than the cousin who resented the direction in which money to which he felt he had a moral claim might be destined—actually was destined—to go? Cause for jealousy—greed with the spur of impecuniosity—opportunity both to plan at leisure and to commit with impunity—all might be proved against Edwin Lovejoy.

To charge Tony Rissole might be to do no more than demonstrate the strength of the case against the real murderer. It might not be merely abortive—it might be ludicrous in its result. Thinking thus, Superintendent Davis was disposed to agree with the inspector's complaint. Every argument in the case had a double edge. The more you built up the case against one, the stronger it became against the alternative criminal. And suppose after all that it was Vestman—the only one of the three who had a previous criminal record—who had struck the blow?

CHAPTER XVII.

A Procedure in Reverse

THE receipt of the draft letter from the American police was followed by a week of tribulation for Chief Inspector Combridge. He toiled seven times as long as the Galilean fishermen, and, like them, he caught nothing at all, though his patient assiduity was to divert Mr. Jellipot from more remunerative occupation on the eighth day.

He questioned Mrs. Lovejoy concerning her relations with the dead man, in a tone he would not have been likely to use but for the allegations which had been made against her. He got no admission at all, and her replies, which seemed slow even to recognize the implications of what he asked, actually raised a doubt in his mind as to how much of exaggeration those imputations might have contained. It was true that when his questions became as pointed as good manners would allow—or even something beyond that elastic boundary—her face had flushed and her eyes had avoided his, but the most experienced investigator might be unsure of the meaning of that. It might be said that a shameless woman would have outfaced him with more assertive denials and bolder eyes. But it might be argued with equal force that one entirely innocent would have been quicker to take offence.

He called at the Aides' also, and found the lady alone. She was one of those women whose natural plainness is not lessened by the approach of mature years. The majority will put on flesh as they admit completing the fourth decade of the cycle of mortal life. Some of them may be scarcely less comely for that. A fortunate minority maintain the slimness and grace of youth, and are to be envied indeed. The remainder become lean and angular. Health may remain, but beauty has left the scene. Mrs. Aide, as she called herself, and as it may be simpler to do, was of the third of these categories. She was tall, thin, bony, and these features were so aggressively present that they would be the distinguishing evidence of her personality which those who met her would retain in mind. Beyond that, she was commonplace rather than abnormal in type. She neither gave the impression of being clever nor stupid. Neither of good character nor of bad. Inspector Combridge was disinclined to consider her as a criminal. She was probably one of those women who drift by mere chance into criminal connections. There are many such who may be led to complicity in evil practices by lovers or relatives, but who may yet have had a restraining rather than a provoking influence upon the events in which they become involved. That is a good reason why they may receive what appears to be unduly lenient comparative treatment when they fall into the hands of the law. Inspector Combridge would readily have believed that the woman's stolid common sense had been a deciding influence in keeping her companion from criminal courses since his brother had died at the hangman's hands.

Now he talked to her very seriously of the imprudence of holding back any information that might be of assistance to the police. She heard him without visible resentment, but with little response. He supposed that he had wasted time, as he often must. Of course, if Vestman were guilty, his advice would have had little value, unless she were prepared to betray the man whose life and business she shared: and equally so if—which seemed the greater probability—she had nothing to tell. He left her, as he had left Mrs. Lovejoy, feeling that he had made no progress at all.

But on the eighth day there was another cable from New York, which read:

> Tony Rissole arrested Baltimore held on minor charge stop do you intend apply extradition stop reply urgent.

Superintendent Davis saw this to be a question which must be referred to the Assistant Commissioner. He cabled back that a reply should be sent within twenty-four hours. The Assistant Commissioner asked for a full written statement of all the evidence against the suspected man on which to base his decision. His intention was to pass this document on to the Home Secretary, so that, if a mistake were made, the funeral should not be his. The document was very promptly prepared, and went on its predestined journey. The following morning, while decision was still delayed, a further cable crossed the Atlantic.

Heavy clasp knife taken from Rissole found clean
except trace human blood within hinge stop arranged
seven days remand stop your decision urgent stop
habeas corpus proceedings threatened to enforce bail.

Superintendent Davis took this cable to the Assistant Commissioner. He found Sir Henry in an irritable mood. He had had a most
polite letter from the Home Office leaving the decision to him. He
had been on the point of deciding to tell his American colleagues
that they could let the man go. He had all along been inclined to
consider Edwin Lovejoy the most probable murderer. And, anyway,
better let the case be added to the list of undiscovered crimes rather
than he should have the blame of a blunder which might become
public, and for which a scapegoat must be found.

But he saw that this fresh fact had a most sinister sound. Waver-
ing in mind, but honestly wishing to do justice to the office he held,
he was tempted to pass on the procedure which had been adopted to
him. Superintendent Davis was a most reliable man. His reputation
was for soundness above everything! Sir Henry said: "Look here,
Davis. You know the case far better than I do. Do what you think
best. I couldn't leave the decision in better hands."

Superintendent Davis said, "Thank you, sir," with no gratitude
in his heart. He added: "Then I'd like to look over the documents
once again."

He didn't really want to do that. He knew them by heart already, as it was his business to do. What he wanted was time to
think.

Sir Henry said: "All right. Here they are." He passed over the
file which had been on his desk since the previous day. "Let me
know what you decide—and, of course, why. I 'd better have a written memo of that."

Even less inclined to gratitude than before, the superintendent
grunted assent, but the eyes of the Assistant Commissioner were already turned to his desk, and his hands moved as one whose attention was returned to more important affairs.

Superintendent Davis went back to his own room. He summoned Combridge for consultation. He said: "They can't make up
their minds what to do. They've passed us the buck."

Inspector Combridge did not look pleased. He thought that
meant that a murderer was to go free, which he disapproved. He had
thought over that last cable, and the traces of human blood left in the
hinge of a knife otherwise carefully cleaned—how commendably
efficient the New York police could be!—seemed decisive to him.

Superintendent Davis saw his expression, and understood. He said: "Yes, I know. But I'm not going to say that I'm not going to decide."

"You're not going to tell me I understand the case better than you?" There was alarm in Inspector Combridge's voice as he made this exclamation. It seemed a low thing for a superior officer to do. And yet—had it not been done twice already? Only, there is a point where such a process is bound to end. To whom could *he* pass it on? It was not easy to see!

But a slow smile creased the superintendent's massive face, and there was a twinkle in the heavy-lidded eyes as he answered the unspoken thought with: "Not exactly that. I thought of letting you get the lawyer's opinion. You seem to think he's right about twelve times to the dozen. He's given us a nasty flop once or twice when he's been on the other side. He might give us a lead now."

"You mean Jellipot?"

"Yes. I mean he. Adrian Rissole was his client. He ought to try make a good guess."

"Then I'll ask if I can see him now."

Mr. Jellipot, being telephoned, said he could be seen any time in the next hour.

Inspector Combridge went to him, and told his tale, excepting only the decisive importance attached to whatever opinion he might be destined to hear.

Mr. Jellipot listened with his usual patient attention. Then he said: "Before we discuss that, I had better tell you that I had a caller yesterday who has some information which may have an important bearing upon your decision. As to that, I am not yet in a position to say. But, had I not been extremely busy since yesterday, I should have rung you up earlier. That is partly why I said I would see you at once when your call came through."

Inspector Combridge settled himself to listen in turn, hoping that, when he had heard, the case might have become clearer than it now was.

But it will be more convenient, even than listening to Mr. Jellipot's lucid statement, to go a few hours backward, to what had passed in his office on the previous day.

CHAPTER XVIII.

The First Interview of the Day Before

WITH a gesture of unusual impatience Mr. Jellipot reached for the telephone. He was engaged upon the drafting of an agreement of exceptional complexity which he had undertaken to have ready during the afternoon, and he had told a new junior clerk that he was not to be lightly disturbed. But the youth, influenced in his inexperience rather by the desire of callers to see the solicitor than any probability that he would be uncontrollably desirous of seeing them, had disturbed him three times already.

"I told you, Jameson," he said sharply, "that I must not be disturbed."

"There's a lady here, sir, who says she must see you most particular."

"Who is she?"

"She won't give any name, sir."

"Then tell her she may have to wait quite a long time. I'm particularly engaged. And don't interrupt me again."

But next moment the bell rang again. "Sorry, sir. But the lady won't wait. She says she doesn't want to be seen here. But I'm to tell you it's something about the Rissole murder."

Mr. Jellipot sighed. Jane Lovejoy, he had no doubt, making a bad guess. Her husband arrested at last, probably on some fresh evidence being procured by Inspector Combridge's indefatigable efforts, and she had hurried to him for help which he must firmly decline to give. But why should she refuse her name? And why should she object to being seen in his office?

Well, a few minutes should be sufficient! He was sorry for her, but the defence of Adrian Rissole's murderer would not be undertaken by him. He said: "Show the lady in."

Next moment he looked up at a woman he did not know, and whom, at the first glance, he saw no reason to like. Perhaps her profession of anonymity was excuse for the fact that he did not rise.

"Please take a seat, madam," he said coldly. "You wish to see me?"

"I wanted to ask your advice."

"Your name is?" He picked up a pencil as though about to record the answer. It was not a cordial reception.

"It would be confidential?"

"I can't possibly say that until I know what your business is."

"I heard from Mrs. Lovejoy that you're interested in the murder of poor Mr. Rissole. I want to ask your advice."

The woman—Mr. Jellipot would have hesitated to endorse Jameson's "lady"—fumbled in her bag. She produced six-and-eight pence, which she laid on Mr. Jellipot's desk. "I believe," she said, "that is the usual fee."

Mr. Jellipot looked at the money without interest. "It sometimes is," he allowed dubiously.

"I want to ask you whether, if anyone gave some information that might help to catch the murderer of Adrian Rissole, they could trust the police not to make it awkward for them?"

Mr. Jellipot's attention was now thoroughly roused, but he gave no sign of any added alertness of mind, or desire to put his visitor at ease.

"As a practising lawyer," he replied, with his usual precision, "I conceive it to be my duty to give the best legal advice which I am able to do to all who approach me with such requests, or to obtain counsel's opinion if I am particularly conscious of my own incompetence. But the question you ask is not a matter of law, but of the prospective conduct of others, under circumstances which are only vaguely indicated. Unless you can be far more explicit, I cannot give you any advice at all. Nor is it a matter on which I could accept the fee which you have tendered, with a punctiliousness that all my clients do not observe." As he concluded this exposition he picked up the money and handed it back.

The tall and angular female who confronted him made no motion to go. She looked undecided. She understood, being of average intelligence, that she had been rebuffed, and that Mr. Jellipot did not intend to curtail his freedom of speech or action by accepting the modest fee she had proffered. But she did not misinterpret this attitude as one of hostility, and she had sense to see that it had an integrity which might make him a safer counsellor, and perhaps confidant, than some solicitors who would have received her in a more affable manner.

"I'd like to tell you," she said, "but it's a thing you can't take back when it's once said. And it isn't me who'd be in the soup; it's someone else, if I'd done wrong. There's someone helped someone a way that it wasn't wise, and he can't let on without giving himself away, more than anyone would be wanting to do. I thought it would be a lot worse for him if it were found out in another way."

"Probably it would. If I should advise you at all, it would be to urge your friend to be frank with the police while there is time, and before they come calling on him. It's almost always the wiser way. But I can't tell you that he would escape any penalty he may have incurred. To be an accessory after such a crime—"

"It wasn't that. It wasn't after. He hadn't any idea—"

"Then I should most strongly urge—but don't you think it would be wiser to tell me what all this is about? It's a matter on which the police might appreciate any help voluntarily given, and, in that direction, I might—but I will promise nothing. You must make your own decision. Don't you think you've gone too far not to tell me now? Adrian Rissole was a client of mine, for whom I had some liking and some respect. I should be personally grateful to anyone who assisted to unravel the mystery of his end."

"I think that's good enough for me. I'm Mrs. Aide. I live—"

"Yes. I know that."

"Well, there was something done for Tony Rissole that must have helped him to get away. If the police knew it, I reckon they'd soon have him in the right place. If they're willing to know it without making trouble for those who tell them—"

"They might be. I suppose it would depend a good deal on what the help would be. But do you mean me to understand that you knew Tony Rissole to have been the murderer?"

Mrs. Aide looked surprised. "I didn't know," she said, "that there was any doubt about that. I should have thought—"

"But the police have been in a considerable doubt, which you may do them a real service if you can remove."

"Oh, the police!" Mrs. Aide's tone was that of one who voices a contempt in which all must concur. "For two pins they'd have said it was us, if they'd known how."

"The police," Mr. Jellipot replied, "sometimes have very difficult duties to perform. And the fallibility of human nature. But it is a subject which I must not pursue now! Suppose I put this matter to them in my own way, and arrange for you to meet Inspector

Combridge here at my office, if I obtain an assurance from him which I think will be satisfactory to you?"

Mrs. Aide did not look happy at this suggestion, but gave a hesitating assent. "We'd better both come, if we come at all. I don't know what Harry'll say to me, breaking in like I've done now. But I've done it more for him than myself. You'd better phone me, if you will, if we're to come. It's Regent 4242."

Mr. Jellipot made a note of this, and as he did so his telephone rang again.

"There's a lady," Jameson's voice informed him, "wants to see you particular. I said you'd have to know what her business was, and she said say it's about Mr. Rissole's murder."

Mr. Jellipot did not even ask his visitor's name on this occasion. With a sigh for the neglected world which lay before him, he answered: "You'd better put her in the waiting room, and show this lady who's with me now out by the other door."

CHAPTER XIX.

THE SECOND INTERVIEW OF THE DAY BEFORE

MRS. AIDE went out by one door, and Mrs. Lovejoy came in by another.

Mr. Jellipot gazed ruefully at the foolscap on his desk, and rose up with more courtesy than he had shown to his previous caller. His judgment of women may not always have equalled that which he applied to his own sex. Rightly or wrongly, be regarded his visitor as one of those who are too weak, intellectually and physically, to control their fates, so that, into whatever trouble they may blunder or drift, they must deserve pity rather than blame. They are set down to the game of life by no choice of theirs, and it is one which they are unequal to play. He might have quoted the parable of the single talent, and said that God Himself would make distinction to require little from such as they.

He saw that his visitor was nervously excited, and while he did not conclude therefrom that she had anything momentous to say—he judged her to be one who might flutter with little cause—he adopted an opposite manner from that with which he had received his previous visitor.

He learned immediately, by a casually worded query as to her husband's welfare, that the ironmonger was still free from Inspector Combridge's detaining hand, and being himself relieved from the apprehension that he might have to resist a woman's plea to undertake the defence of a probably guilty man, he became cheerfully platitudinous in such preliminary exchange of conversation as would be likely to put her at ease of mind, while sunk in the physical comfort of a well-padded and ample chair.

Jane Lovejoy, being sensitive to atmosphere, as women of her type commonly are, responded readily to this treatment. Her nervous tension relaxed. "I wanted," she said, in a timid voice, which might gain confidence with the encouragement it was likely to meet, "to ask you to do something for me."

Mr. Jellipot heard this opening without surprise. She was the sort of woman who goes through life asking for help. Nor, though habitual caution withheld him from any word of assent, did he feel disinclined to do anything in his power, short of defending a guilty man. Flushed and troubled as she was, her shallow prettiness, which had a quality of immaturity it would not easily lose, showed at its best. Mr. Jellipot was not too easily influenced by such observations, but he was conscious of an inclination, paternal rather than amative, to assist his present visitor which his previous one had not inspired.

"Perhaps," he said, "you'd better tell me the whole tale."

Mrs. Lovejoy did not deny that there was a tale to be told before her request could be intelligently advanced, but she evidently found it hard to begin. She twisted a damp handkerchief in her hand, for which it seemed likely that there would be further use.

Mr. Jellipot considered that Edwin Lovejoy was almost certain to have some part in any tale that would come from his wife's lips. He aimed obliquely to lead her first step on a difficult road when he said: "I had some anticipation that both you and your husband would have found life go more happily now that your financial troubles are ended. "

"Yes," she answered vaguely, "yes—of course—it's much better now."

Her tone was without satisfaction in what she said. It encouraged him to continue: "But there is some trouble that still remains?"

"Yes. It's between Edwin and me. And I don't know—I don't know what I ought to do."

Mr. Jellipot had heard many previous narrations of matrimonial trouble from occupants of the chair in which Mrs. Lovejoy sat. Some of them had seemed very trivial to him, even absurd, such as sensible people would face and reconcile in ten minutes of straightforward talk; but he had learnt the delusion of this apparent simplicity. To one who regarded a lawyer's work as akin to that of a physician, so that, whatever its profit might be to him, it would be a record of failure unless those whom he undertook to serve should go away healed and comforted, there would be few subjects requiring more anxious thought.

"Well," he said in his kindliest manner, "such things sometimes seem less serious to others than to those who are most concerned; and when they are talked over frankly, they often disappear altogether."

"Do you think so?" she said eagerly. "I expect you know best!" But then her voice fell flatly to: "Only it's not as simple as that!"

"If you would tell me just what the trouble is?"

"Edwin," she said, the words coming in a sudden rush of confidence, "isn't sure that I didn't know more of Adrian than he'd thought I did. And he isn't sure that I'm not sure that he didn't guess it before, and kill him because of that. And we've got so that we look at each other and never talk. And he didn't like it when I cleaned the knives, though it was what he said, or I shouldn't have thought of that. And I've got so frightened I can't sleep."

Mr. Jellipot's mind, working in its usual methodical manner, fastened on the solitary objective fact which this emotional outburst bore. "Mr. Lovejoy," he questioned, "asked you to clean the knives?"

"Yes," she began, "it was after—" But then she stopped abruptly. Her face whitened. She made a motion to rise, pushing the wet handkerchief into her bag. "I haven't made you think Edwin did it?" she asked in a frightened voice. "If I'd thought you could think that—"

"No," Mr. Jellipot answered, his voice soothing her, as his outstretched hand inclined her to remain seated. "No. I am disposed towards a different explanation." He was conscious, as he said this, that he was influenced by the declaration of his previous caller—which he had not had opportunity to subject to the analysis of a slow-working mind, and which, apart from that, was little more as yet than a promise of revelations to come. But the evidence against Tony Rissole was already formidable and of growing weight. Yes, he told himself in a scrupulous mind, he had said no more than was true—but why had Edwin Lovejoy been anxious that she should clean the knives?

This was no more than instantaneous inarticulate thought, for her next words arrested his attention sharply. "You mean," she said, in a relieved voice, "that you know it was Tony?" and then added: "It was nothing about the knives. I left them dirty. Edwin's always at me for that. It was rabbit's blood."

Mr. Jellipot had ceased to be interested in the knives. He asked: "You knew about Tony Rissole? Why should you think it was he?"

"Of course it was him. Who else would it be likely to be?"

"You mustn't expect me to answer that. And that isn't quite the way to begin. The first questions are why you should think it was Tony, and what motive he could have had."

"Well, he took all the money there was in the flat, didn't he? And Adrian used to keep a lot there."

"You know that as a fact?"

"Yes. I saw it. About eighty pounds. That's what he said it was. It looked more."

"How did you come to see it?"

"Because he wanted to give it to me."

"But you wouldn't take it?"

"No. It wouldn't have been any use. Edwin would have had it for the business. It would all have gone the same way. But," she added, in a burst of candour, such as became easy as she watched Mr. Jellipot's sympathetic and understanding eyes, "it wasn't really that. I was scared to death. I thought if Edwin knew I had money from him, he'd be certain to wonder why."

"So you never had any of Adrian's money, though he offered to lend—or perhaps give—it?"

"I never had anything much. I had to buy myself clothes. Edwin never noticed that." There was a note of resentment in her voice, weakly bitter, as she said this. "And Edwin liked a good meal when he got home at night. And when I was afraid to order from Joliff's, and daren't even pass Bridgewater's shop—"

"Yes. I think I can understand. But what is it you want me to do?"

"I want you to tell Edwin everything. I've tried twice, but I didn't dare. I want you to make him understand that it didn't mean anything much. And that, anyhow, it was his fault more than a bit. And that I don't think he killed Adrian. And that I want things to go on as they were before."

"Yes. It might be wise. I can't say till I know more than I do now. Do I understand rightly that your relations with Adrian Rissole were on a footing of—considerable familiarity?"

"Yes. They were—well, what you'd suppose. I'd got nothing else to do."

"And your husband had no suspicion of that?"

"Not before Adrian died. Not the least. He was thinking too much about other things." The tone of weak resentment came again with these words. "He doesn't really believe there was anything now—not anything much. Only it's hateful the way he looks, now he's not sure."

Mr. Jellipot understood that too. He knew that uncertainty may be worse than knowledge. A thing may be forgiven, especially if it be ended beyond possibility of repetition. But if you are less than sure, you cannot even forgive; and forgetting becomes a more difficult feat. "And you are sure," he asked, "that you want me to tell Mr. Lovejoy this?"

Jane Lovejoy's handkerchief had come out again. She twisted it in her hands as she replied: "Yes. If you would. I shan't have any peace till he knows. I thought you might make him understand that it never meant anything much. And that I'm sorry for what I did. I thought you might make him see it the right way. "

It was the kind of statement which had been heard more than once before in the solicitor's office, revealing the unconscious self-ishness of the type of mind from which it would come.

He recalled the case of a man who had confided to him that he had embezzled money from his employer seventeen years before. He said that his conscience would give him no peace until he had con-fessed his crime and given himself up to the police. He had a crude idea that if he were punished by his fellow men he would be more likely to escape a divine judgment to follow, and so, with no better motive than that, he was willing to lose his position, bring his family to shame and poverty, and put his neighbours to pointless expense and trouble. It took Mr. Jellipot two hours of patient reasoning to convince the man of the base folly of what he had been proposing to do.

But this was a somewhat different matter. If Jane Lovejoy's ac-count were to be believed, suspicion already stirred. Under such cir-cumstances silence might be a poor foundation on which to build for the happiness of future years. That was if her fear were correct. It was at least equally possible that it was the imagination of a timid and guilty mind. And there was another possibility. Suppose that Edwin Lovejoy, when alone with his wife, was disposed to brood over the memory of a dreadful crime, and the fear that there would be discovery of his guilt? Might not she, with her own guilty secret upon her mind, misinterpret his moody ways?

Considering these possibilities, Mr. Jellipot avoided the imme-diate issue. Seeking to obtain the fullest data on which to base his decision, he recalled that she had not explained her knowledge of Tony Rissole, which was something her husband had not shared, unless there had been a lack of frankness on his part for which no reason appeared. Mr. Jellipot recalled the tale of the "seaman" whom he had met on the stairs, and whose face he had failed to see, but whom he might recognize again by other items of his appear-ance. That was scarcely consistent with his having encountered a man he already knew.

"Before I can undertake what you ask," he said cautiously— "which I do not refuse," he added hastily, seeing her face changing to an aspect portending tears—"I must understand the whole posi-tion more clearly than I do now. You speak of Tony Rissole as of a man you knew, and who would be capable of such a crime. Does your husband share this opinion?"

"Edwin doesn't know anything about it. I don't think he ever heard Tony's name, unless it's from you or Mr. Combridge."

"He certainly hasn't heard it from me. I cannot tell what Inspector Combridge may have said. But if you knew of him before, didn't you identify him with the seafaring man that your husband says he passed on the stairs?"

"Yes. Of course it was. Who else could it have been?"

"And you naturally explained this probability to Mr. Lovejoy?"

Jane Lovejoy looked more confused than she had done at any time during the voluntary confessions which she had already made.

"No, I haven't said anything about that."

"But surely it would have been a most natural thing to do?"

"Well, I—I just didn't."

"I think," Mr. Jellipot said gently, but in a tone of firm finality, "that you must have had a better reason than that."

"Well, I hadn't mentioned him before. Edwin might have thought it seemed queer."

"You mean that you had not been confidential about what went on during the day in Adrian Rissole's flat, including one or more occasions when Tony had been there?"

"Yes," she said, in a relieved voice, "that was just it."

Mr. Jellipot had a moment of silence. He pondered this ready admission, and decided that it left much more to be said. How, from such casual encounter with a man whose visits to Adrian Rissole were brief, infrequent, and unwelcome, could she have formed so confident an opinion that Tony would be the man 'to put a knife in his cousin's back?' But perhaps her estimate of the sea carpenter's character came less from personal observation than opinions or even fears that Adrian had confided to her?

"You had better tell me," he said, "what you saw of Tony Rissole, and why you formed such a bad opinion of him."

"Oh, anyone would! He was a horrible man." She paused, and then, as Mr. Jellipot remained expectantly silent, she added, in an incoherent rush of words: "You'd better know. I—went out—with him once. I couldn't again. Not for anything. He wasn't nice. Not in his ways. He was a horrible man. And then, when I wouldn't, he said he'd tell Edwin about something he'd seen going on between Adrian and me, and Adrian wanted to give him money to go away, and I said there'd be no end to that, and I'd tell him he could say anything he liked to Edwin because there was nothing he didn't know, and he didn't care what I did, and so I told him that, and made him believe more or less, and he said that was all the more reason I shouldn't be awkward about going with him, and I said I supposed I could go with who I liked, and it wasn't him, and Adrian said that if he frightened me anymore he wouldn't ever get a penny of his, not while he was alive or when he was dead, and he went away swearing what he'd do to us both when he came again, if we didn't dance to another tune.

"But, of course," she ended on a quieter note, "I didn't tell Edwin this: it wasn't likely I should."

"You say he made threats of personal violence against both yourself and Adrian? Can you remember accurately what he said?"

"Not to repeat. It was just swearing, and words that I didn't know. They didn't sound like things that he'd really do. Just to frighten us, I supposed. And Adrian took no notice of them at all. He didn't even trouble to answer back. Oh, I remember one thing. He said he'd cut the guts out of us both. He said that more than once."

"It was a threat," Mr. Jellipot considered, "not, as you rightly felt, to be taken with literality. You may have been correct in regarding them as little more than the ravings of an angry man who had not cultivated a high standard of verbal exactitude. But they showed the spirit from which crimes of violence are born. You would be prepared, if necessary, to swear in a public court that such threats were used?"

Mrs. Lovejoy's eyes opened widely in a frightened face. "Oh," she exclaimed, "but that's just what I don't want to do! It's being afraid of that that's made me come here in the way I have. At least, it's that as much as anything else. Why, Edwin would hear it all if I did that. He'd hear it in a dreadful way!"

Mr. Jellipot judged, as he heard this, that her tale had been fully told. He did not see how Mrs. Lovejoy could reasonably have feared that Tony Rissole's threats would have been publicly disclosed unless she should reveal them herself, but he saw that she might have cause for a vaguer fear that, if he should be placed in the dock, her relations with one or both of the two men might not be safe from exposure, in the course of that deadly ordeal of life and death.

As to his own course, he was not inclined to refuse help, but he must not decide too hastily what his advice or action should be.

"You had better," he said, "leave me to think this over. I will promise you that, if your husband should ever learn of these unfortunate events, it will not be in a public court."

She went off with no more than this limited assurance, but looking much happier than when she had entered the solicitor's office.

She felt that her troubles had been taken into kindly and very capable hands.

Mr. Jellipot, reflecting upon the confession which he had heard, decided that the case against Tony Rissole gained a convincing strength.

It was true that he would have been unlikely to murder his cousin had he known that it would lead to Jane Lovejoy's inheriting the whole estate. But he could have had no knowledge of the existence of such a will, nor serious fear that it had been already made, or he would surely have made an exhaustive search. He might have struck the blow in the hope that he would inherit all, as the next of kin of an intestate deceased. Certainly, the sooner Adrian were dead the less risk there would be that he would have willed his property away from its natural heir. And, added to that, there might have been the motive of immediate robbery. Greed—hate—revenge—there was no light measure of motive here!

It was with this tale, and Mrs. Aide's promised disclosure on his mind, that he met Chief Inspector Combridge on the next day.

CHAPTER XX.

Mr. Jellipot Makes His Choice

MR. JELLIPOT weighed his words with care, as it was his habit to do. Inspector Combridge had not embarrassed him with the knowledge that his advice was to be accepted as decisive, but he had made it clear that it was that to which he would be glad to listen.

Yet he was in less hesitation than when he had entered the solicitor's office, for the additional information he now heard, dovetailing into that which had come from New York, seemed to him to be sufficient to put doubt aside, even without the further revelation which Vestman might be able to make.

Now he heard Mr. Jellipot's opinion with satisfaction, as confirming that which he had already formed.

"The facts we have," the solicitor said, "are not proof, and if I were on a jury before which they were laid as they now stand, I should decline to convict upon them, though there might be many to call me wrong. But, at least, there is a strong presumption of guilt. Apart from certain reasons of suspicion of Edwin Lovejoy, they would appear to most people to be of a conclusive quality.

"But the case against Edwin Lovejoy differs in some important particulars. There was motive. There was opportunity. The motive—possibly two motives—were very strong. The opportunity was ample. But there the case against him entirely ends. There is no concrete circumstance of any kind which connects him with the crime. It might be regarded—if we assume Tony Rissole's guilt—as an almost perfect example of how treacherous circumstantial deduction may be

"It is true that the case against Tony Rissole is circumstantial also, but there are important distinctions. There is evidence both of verbal and written threats. To certain motive, and presumable opportunity, inclination is added, which is a most important supplement. There is no evidence that such a thought even entered Edwin

101

Lovejoy's mind, or that he would have given consideration to it. That is, of course, merely negative in its character, but it is a distinction to be observed.

"Then there is a difference between the subsequent conduct of the two men. Edwin Lovejoy held his ground. It is true that it would have been extremely foolish for him, if guilty, to have attempted flight. Again, this evidence is negative, or even negligible, in itself. But the conduct of Tony Rissole is of a more affirmative kind. It may be capable of explanation, which should be fairly considered; but, in the absence of such explanation, it has the aspects of folly and guilt.

"Finally, and perhaps most damning of all, there is the trace of human blood in the knife's hinge.

"There must be many ways in which a knife blade may be stained with human blood, some of which are quite innocent; and such blood will suppose, most often be that of the one to whom the knife belongs. But in the great majority of such cases the blood would have been on the blade alone. For it to have reached the hinge implies, with approximate certainty, that it had drenched the knife— a seaman's knife, I suppose; of substantial size—as the blood of Adrian Rissole must have done to whatever weapon inflicted that cruel wound.

"Tony Rissole would have had ample opportunities to remove any other bloodstains, or to destroy the clothes on which they appeared. He would naturally clean his knife. He would clean it with care. But, having done so, he might naturally think it more prudent to keep it than to throw it away, and perhaps have to explain its loss.

"Such a knife is, I believe, a customary article for such men to have: there would be no ground for suspicion in that.

"I have said that he would clean it with care. He would doubtless think that all traces of his victim's blood had been thoroughly cleansed away. But with modern methods of microscopic examination and analysis, that there were remaining traces of blood in the hinge would be exactly what I should have expected to hear."

"And yet," Inspector Combridge commented, as Mr. Jellipot paused, as though dwelling inwardly upon his own lucid analysis, "if you were on the jury, you'd rather give us one in the eye than see the fellow get what he deserves."

"Did I say that? Perhaps I may have been less than clear. As the case stands, I should say it is less than proof, though not much. But it seems to me to warrant an arrest, and I should suppose that—if he be a guilty man—his efforts to explain and defend himself will be conclusive in their results. And there is the information which the

Aides are able to give, which we may fairly expect, whatever it be, to strengthen the case you already have."

"It looks as though I shall be taking a trip to New York on to-morrow's boat."

"It should be a pleasant interlude to a busy life."

"I don't know about that. The best thing I know about the sea is the pleasure you feel when the time comes to get off the boat. But there's one side of the case we shall have to handle carefully. I mean about Mrs. Lovejoy. It might easily be twisted to bring Edwin Lovejoy in—at least enough to give the jury a doubt we shouldn't want them to have. What sort of witness do you think she's likely to make?"

Mr. Jellipot did not find this question easy to answer. He had not communicated all the confidences which he had received from Jane Lovejoy on the previous day, but having been told of the allegations made by the Misses Ranger, and implied in the draft letter which had been taken from Tony Rissole's room, he had felt free to state that, on her own admission, they were substantially justified.

"I shouldn't," he said now, "describe her as one who would be likely to prove a good witness, as we lawyers are disposed—perhaps wrongly—to use that adjective. She is not one who could be trusted to tell a tale already rehearsed, neither more nor less. I should describe her as—well, as an inadequate woman.

"But she is one of those from whose confused statements the truth is likely to emerge in convincing ways. If you desire that a jury shall learn the truth, neither more nor less, I should say she'll be a very good witness indeed."

"You mean if we've got a good case she'll be good for us, and, if not, she'll let us down with a bang?"

"That is substantially what I meant. And it is, I suppose, what we should all wish to occur. But before you finally decide to bring Tony Rissole back, might it not be well to hear what Vestman may have to say?"

"Yes. If we can get hold of him at once. But it's a matter that can't wait."

"Then I will see what can be done." Saying this, Mr. Jellipot picked up his telephone and gave instructions that he should be put through to the number which Mrs. Aide had given him on the previous day.

CHAPTER XXI.

WHAT VESTMAN HAD TO TELL

MRS. AIDE would not go to Scotland Yard. Neither would her husband. She was explicit on that. Anything further which might be said must be in Mr. Jellipot's presence, or it would not be spoken at all. And her husband would be with her. She had talked it over with him, and he was prepared to help the police, but it was clear that he felt in a position to bargain, and meant to do so.

Chief Inspector Combridge did not look pleased. He said something about living to see him laugh on the other side of his mouth, to which expression Mr. Jellipot gave a moment of puzzled thought, and passed it by for more exigent considerations. But the inspector, having revealed his feelings by that expletive, put them aside in recognition of temporal urgency, and said he would meet the pair there, if they would come at once.

This being agreed, he came to a belated consciousness that he was making a somewhat free use of Mr. Jellipot's office and time. But the solicitor said, with logic enough, that as he himself had been the medium of fixing the appointment, he had no title to complain, provided only that Inspector Combridge would kindly wait in another room, so that he could deal with other appointments until the Aides should arrive?

So it was done, and in less than an hour the ex-burglar and his presumptive wife were seated, with no appearance of ease, in Mr. Jellipot's office.

"You've got something," Inspector Combridge began, with some abruptness, "you want to tell me about Tony Rissole—something you knew, and didn't tell me before?"

"I don't want to tell you anything," the man answered. "I don't want to get mixed up in it at all. But if I do, there's something I want to ask first, and be clear on that."

"I shan't make any promises in the dark," Inspector Combridge answered firmly, "so if you want that you're wasting time. But if you're frank with us you'll get the best treatment the law allows, and it's a lot wiser to tell us first than leave us to find out in another way, especially if you've been what we call an accessory after the fact, as I'm expecting to hear."

"I haven't been an accessory to anything before or after," the man answered, and then corrected himself to add: "not about the murder, anyhow. I knew nothing about that, and I don't now. But what I'm wanting to do is to change my name in a legal way. I've been wanting to do that for a long time, but I didn't know what it might bring up. But now you know who I am, I want to do it, if I can make sure that the police won't interfere in the wrong way."

This was a species of bargain that the inspector had not expected to hear proposed. He felt a momentary uncertainty as to the reply which he ought to give, concerning a matter on which he had no authority to pledge the action of his superior officers, nor could he recall a precedent to guide his judgment.

As he paused, Mr. Jellipot interposed. "I suspect," he said, "that you are asking far more than Inspector Combridge, on his own authority, can undertake, and you will recognize that it is one on which I have none at all. But I think I can tell you that, you being a man of English birth, and against whom, if I am correctly informed, no criminal conviction has been recorded, there would be no probability that the police would, or even could, obstruct you in the making of such a change. But, be that as it may, you can lose nothing in that direction by assisting them in the course of justice now."

The man looked doubtfully at the woman who sat silently at his side. "It's the best way, Harry," she said. "You'd better do it how Mr. Jellipot says." Her only anxiety appeared to be that Vestman should not take offence, or fail to propitiate the dreadful force of the law.

"I dare say that's right enough," he said, "but I'd want to know something beyond that. I want to know that what I say won't be followed up to make trouble for me or anyone else. That's not much to ask. There's no sense"—he turned directly to Inspector Combridge as he said this—"in helping you if I'm to get nothing for it, or even some trouble I might miss if I let things rest as they are."

"I haven't understood yet," the inspector answered, "what help you'd be able to give."

"Suppose I could put you on to how Tony got away, so that you'd know where you'd be likely to find him now?"

"I'm not going to promise you anything if you helped him to get away."

"I didn't do anything at the time of the murder. It all happened last year. But it might put you on his track now."

"If that's all you've got, it's no use to us. We're on his track right enough. He's under arrest."

"Then you'll want no more help from me."

As the man said this, he rose abruptly, an action for which a note of curtness in the inspector's voice may have been even more responsible than the information that it conveyed. The woman raised a restraining hand to his arm, but it had no more effect than to cause him to stand irresolutely. "It's no use, Bessie," he said, "we're wasting time, if not worse. And from what I've just heard I should say we can get what we want without this."

Chief Inspector Combridge was conscious that his diplomacy had not been beyond criticism. It was true that Tony was under arrest, but he was by no means indifferent to obtaining further information concerning his movements during the past weeks. He said: "You won't be going a very good way about it if you begin by refusing to give us information about a man who's under a charge of murder."

"Not when two people here have heard you say it wouldn't be any use to you?" the man sneered, to which the baffled inspector was not quick to make effective reply.

Mr. Jellipot's quiet leisurely voice took control of the situation again. "I don't think Inspector Combridge meant exactly that. It might help him a great deal to know what Tony's movements were after he left the flat."

"Then he must find out some other way. I can't tell him what I don't know."

"But," Mr. Jellipot suggested with gentle persistence, "you could tell something which would help us to find out what those movements were."

"I haven't said that."

"No. But you haven't denied it, now, which comes to much the same thing."

"I don't see how you make that out." (Mr. Jellipot himself had a distressing doubt as to whether he had not transgressed the limit of abstract logic, but it was not a time for weighing that in a scrupulous mind, as he had an inclination to do.) "It wasn't anything that happened round about now. It was last year. It might help now, or it might not."

"I expect it would," Mr. Jellipot said hopefully. "It's wonderful what Inspector Combridge will do, following up some little fact that would have no meaning for me at all."

"You'd better tell them, Harry," the woman said again. It was clear that she had her own reason for wishing the interview to end on a better note than it threatened to have, and that he was under the influence of her stubborn persistent will.

"I'm not going to get anyone into trouble," he said sullenly, as though he only now realized the full consequences of what he was being persuaded to do, but it was a note of yielding, however reluctantly He added, a moment later: "It was no more than wanting to have a passport what he could use if he ever got in a bad jam."

"And you put him up to where he could get it?" Inspector Combridge suggested.

"I haven't said that."

"It seems to me," Mr. Jellipot interposed, observing the effect which any words from Inspector Combridge had on this voluntary and yet reluctant witness, "that it doesn't matter who assisted him to get what he required, if we have the fact of what he was able to do. We may assume that the passport was to be in—shall we say in a borrowed name?"

Vestman answered yes to that, with more amiability in his voice than his replies to the inspector had shown; and that astute officer became silent, leaving the conversation to Mr. Jellipot's gentle but tenacious guidance.

"And I suppose he got what he wanted without much difficulty?"

"Yes. It's only a matter of what you're willing to pay. Everyone knows that."

"We are all apt," Mr. Jellipot reflected aloud, "to assume that our own knowledge is a common property, and that equally few are conversant with matters of which we are not informed. I must confess that, until a few days ago, I was unaware that there is a market in which such passports can be obtained. But we may consider it to be no more than a natural if not necessary consequence of the restriction upon human liberty which these instruments impose."

Mr. Aide, or Vestman, did not follow this reflection clearly. The language was not his, and such words as "instrument" confused rather than elucidated; but he recognized the aloof impartiality of Mr. Jellipot's attitude as being very different from that of the inspector, who was more concerned to enforce than criticize an existing law; and when the solicitor added, "But as it is agreed that Tony Rissole obtained, with whatever object, one of these somewhat fictitious credentials, it appears to me that all we require further is the name which appeared upon it," he answered readily, though scarcely to the satisfaction of those who heard: "I reckoned you'd ask that, and I don't say it can't be found out, though it won't be easy, and it may be that there's no record at all."

"But you will do your best to obtain this information for us?"

"I'll have a good try, if it's agreed that I shan't get anyone into any trouble, and if I'm not followed about."

"I feel sure that Inspector Combridge will agree to those conditions."

"Well, it wouldn't be easy to set a watch on me that I didn't spot, and if I did I shouldn't move anymore. Not a foot for all the promises you could make. Of course, there'll be something to pay."

"You mean that you hope to obtain this information from someone who will expect remuneration?"

"Yes. That's sense, isn't it? You can't expect anyone who knows to let the police have it free. They wouldn't give much to him. Not the sort of thing he'd be glad to have."

"Would ten pounds be enough?"

"Yes. I dare say it would. But I can't say. I can't say that I can get it at all."

"Oh, but I feel sure that you will. I don't think you're the man to fail. And I promise you there will be ten pounds to be had here any time in exchange for the name on the passport that Tony bought."

Vestman said that that was good enough for him. He was always willing to take a gentleman's word. He rose to go, saying that he would get to work at once.

But before he went he paused to obtain Inspector Combridge's own assurance that he would be left with a free hand in the matter, and that no one should incur any penalty through his half-exposure of this illicit transaction.

Not very willingly, but in sufficiently explicit words, the required undertaking was given; and Vestman left with a promise to return to Mr. Jellipot's office as soon as he should have any information to report.

The woman, with a deferential "Good afternoon, sir" to Mr. Jellipot, and a less confident mutter in Inspector Combridge's direction, followed the ex-burglar, with a satisfied expression upon her angular features.

She knew what she wanted, and meant to have. She was expecting a child. She was resolved that she should be married to Vestman, and that it should be in a name which he was legally entitled to use.

They could not abandon that of Aide, by which they were known among too many business and private acquaintances. She had little knowledge either of the legal conditions under which names may be changed, or the validity of marriage in an assumed name. But she meant to avoid the risks which ignorance should be slow to take.

She was convinced that Vestman had had no part in the murder, nor any subsequent knowledge of it. But she had seen that if Tony Rissole should be arrested with the faked passport upon him, and should say where he had bought it, it would be readily believed by the police, who might go on to enquire concerning the names and declarations used by Vestman and herself when they had returned to England. It was a danger which could be avoided, if at all, by going to the police before there should be any more visits from them.

So she had resolved, and, having had her way, she was satisfied by the result. Inspector Combridge had been rather nasty. But nastiness is to be expected from such a source. And Mr. Jellipot was one you could trust. The path of respectability had not been easy for her, but she felt that she had added an upward step to others which she had taken before.

CHAPTER XXII.

TONY IS FOR THE DOCK

"I SUPPOSE that clinches it," Inspector Combridge remarked as the door closed.

"I am inclined," Mr. Jellipot responded cautiously, "to the same opinion. The fact, taken by itself, that a man already free to travel in his own name should go to the expense, and legal risk, of providing himself with a fictitious passport, suggests that he was even then contemplating the possibility that he might be engaged in some criminal action which would render expedient an anonymous flight. And if it can be shown that he made use of this passport to return to New York immediately after the date on which the murder occurred, it will be a most important addition to the evidence which you have already obtained."

Inspector Combridge said with emphasis that it certainly would.

"At the same time," Mr. Jellipot continued, with that invincible habit of exhaustive analysis which was apt to irritate those who prefer to fit their arguments to a single scale, "we must not fail to observe that it was a particularly abortive expedient, in view of the fact that he could not have intended to make a permanent disappearance, unless he were prepared to sacrifice his claim to the estate of the murdered man; and that, as his coming to England could be easily traced and proved, he was drawing suspicion, rather than diverting it from himself, by creating a mystery as to how he had returned to America, for which he might find it very difficult to give an alternative and credible explanation."

"They don't think it out like that." Inspector Combridge spoke from an experienced mind. "They just get funky and bolt."

"I have no doubt you are right. I presume that you will now decide to take a berth on tomorrow's boat?"

"No. I don't think I shall. I shall ask for someone else to be sent over to bring him back. Anyone can do that. I should like to follow up this question of how he went."

"I suppose—unless the illicit passport should be found in his possession—that the value of the information you now have will depend almost entirely upon whether Vestman can supply you with the name upon it?"

"Oh, I couldn't say that. But of course it will have been destroyed. Any mug would throw it away when he got ashore, having used it in the way he had. If Vestman can't get us the name, we shall have to go over the passenger lists and verify them. We could make a list of the doubtful passengers and show Rissole's photo to the cabin stewards who waited upon them. They usually remember them longer than this when they've made their beds for a week. We should just have to work backwards. It might be slow, but it ought to get us home in the end."

Mr. Jellipot thought, not for the first time, that he was glad he was not on the staff of the C.I.D. He said: "But I suppose you won't try that elaborate method unless you give up hope that Vestman will do what you require?"

"Oh, I don't know. Time means a lot in a case like this. I'll tell you what I will do. I'll have an alphabetical list compiled of all passengers who sailed for the United States or Canada (we mustn't forget that) during the week after the murder, and strike them off as we verify the particulars that the steamship companies' records show. It wouldn't be such a long list when we've boiled it down. And we can omit the first class. He wouldn't try that. He'd be making himself too conspicuous. And besides—well, he wouldn't."

"No, I should say you are right there."

"And steerage wouldn't be likely. Not for one who knows the ropes, as he would. The steerage passports get more attention than those in the higher grades, and landing isn't so simple. He'd go tourist, it's three to one.

"Anyway, you shall have the list, when it's weeded out, and then, if Vestman comes in with a name for us to buy, you can look it down. And if the man's there, you can hand him the tenner—a banknote will be the best—and, if it isn't, you can tell him to call again on the next day."

"I don't think," Mr. Jellipot replied, "that he will bring us the wrong name. But it is a list which I shall be pleased to have before me if he should call. And now, if you will excuse me, I must turn my attention to other matters."

Inspector Combridge left at this hint, and, on returning to Superintendent Davis's office, had no difficulty in convincing that cautious officer, even apart from Mr. Jellipot's opinion, that they now had sufficient justification for applying for the extradition of Tony Rissole.

With this decision he put the possibility of Edwin Lovejoy's guilt definitely aside. It might still be necessary to bring the case against Tony Rissole to stricter proof than it now had: it was true that he would not be officially guilty unless and until twelve of his fellow countrymen had expressed that unanimous opinion, but in the eyes of the C.I.D. he was the murderer of Adrian Rissole, and to secure his conviction by every legitimate means had become the simple duty of all concerned.

Mr. Jellipot, with more detachment of mind, was inclined to the same conclusions. He had not absolutely rejected the possibility that Adrian Rissole might have died from the thrust of an ironmonger's knife, but he had relegated it to the category of improbabilities on which men of discretion decline to act. Had it been Edwin Lovejoy whom it was proposed to extradite, it is certain that he would have condemned such a procedure with exhaustive analysis.

Now, when he thought of the tenant of the top flat of Barclays Buildings, it was less as a potential murderer than as one involved in a conjugal difficulty with which he had undertaken to deal.

He examined this problem in an experienced mind, and had some hope that he would not fail. He was not cynical by disposition, but he had been a practising lawyer for more years than he was careful to count, and he knew that money can be potent in many ways. Jane Lovejoy had the money now. If her husband should divorce her he would be left in a very unenviable position. Considering other emotional factors, he saw that, whether guilty or innocent, the man must be disturbed by the suspicion which had been raised against him. If he should be relieved of this by the conviction of Tony Rissole, as he was already relieved of the financial clouds which had darkened his recent days, he might be persuaded without much difficulty to condone offences which were so definitely of the past, and of which the participants would be dead—the one murdered, and the other hanged for the deed.

Mr. Jellipot saw that it might be advantageous to choose a moment for the vicarious confession he had undertaken to make when the ironmonger would be most conscious of these reliefs, but he must remember his promise to Mrs. Lovejoy that the facts should not be first disclosed in a public court. He saw that his choice of time might have to be narrowly made.

But while he felt that he had undertaken an operation which must be delicately performed, he had little anxiety as to its results. He did not think the bond between the Lovejoys to be very strong, but he knew that a slack rope is the less likely to snap.

He knew that there are many ideal marriages—a surprisingly large number considering that most women, if they have choice at all, must make it among comparatively few men, and that there are many thousands of others, any one of whom they would marry with equal or greater willingness if the opportunity should be theirs. But, having married, what they make of it depends mainly upon themselves.

Between the Lovejoys there might never be any spiritual intimacy, or more than superficial understandings, but it was evident that the woman, whatever her levities of conduct might have been, regarded her marriage as a static condition which it would be disaster to end. So far, so good. Mr. Jellipot thought that there would be little difficulty in showing her husband the advantages of this attitude.

One question remained. Would that be best for the woman also? She might have the timidity of disposition which disinclined her to face a crisis, which would sacrifice more permanent things to avoid what she would call the "unpleasantness" of an angry scene. But might it not be his duty to advise her in an opposite way? On the whole, he thought not. It was true she had become financially independent. But, for a single woman of her limitations, there might be added peril in that. Married to Edwin Lovejoy, she would at least have the security of a husband who would not waste or gamble her little fortune away. (It was less certain that he might not sink it in a continuation of his stubbornly impossible fight with opponents who carried more guns than he, but Mr. Jellipot thought that there might be a means of turning that danger aside.) There remained only the possibility that Jane Lovejoy might be a murderer's wife. If he were seriously doubtful of that.... But he had decided differently. He felt that, having formed that deliberate judgment, he must act consistently with it. But he owned to himself that his assurance was less than absolute. He was certain now that, if Edwin Lovejoy had committed the crime, it was a deed of which his wife had no guilty knowledge before or since, and he felt *almost* sure that he was an innocent man. He would not go beyond that.

For the moment there was nothing to be done except to await the promised communication from Mr. Aide. But the days passed, and lengthened into a week, and nothing more was heard from that direction.

A long list of names of trans-Atlantic passengers whose passports were not above possible challenge now lay on Mr. Jellipot's desk, as the result of Inspector Combridge's exhaustive enquiries. The newspapers announced that Tony Rissole was being brought back to his native land in the custody of Inspector Tong. But Mr. Jellipot still replied to the daily telephone enquiry from Scotland Yard that he had heard nothing further from Mr. Aide. Did he not think that something ought to be done? No, he did not. Keeping his word was a habit he did not intend to break without much more than the present cause.

CHAPTER XXIII.

MR. JELLIPOT FINDS THAT ADMIRATION CAN GO TOO FAR

IT appeared that Mr. Jellipot's patience was justified when a morning came on which, while listening impassively to the arguments of two agitated business men who were endeavouring to persuade him that there was no occasion for the London & Northern Bank to appoint a receiver of the business which they directed more obviously to their own profit than that of their creditors, he was interrupted by a telephone call from Mrs. Aide.

"I am," he said at once in explanatory warning, "engaged in a business consultation, but I shall be pleased to listen to anything you may have to say."

"Harry wanted me to tell you that it hasn't been easy to arrange, but he's done it now. He wants you to post me a cheque here, to the Dean Street address. He says ten pounds will be enough. He wants it sent in a plain envelope, addressed to the firm—Aide & Co. It's not to be notes. It's to be a crossed cheque made out to him—Mr. Henry Aide."

"That," Mr. Jellipot said, "shall have my attention in the next hour."

He would have liked to say more, but the occasion was not opportune. When he had leisure for thought, he was intrigued by the apparent contradiction of the caution which stipulated that the money should be sent in a plain envelope to the Aides' Dean Street address, and that it should be in the form of a crossed cheque, the passage and clearance of which would be permanently recorded.

He mentioned this with particularity when he narrated the incident to Superintendent Davis, who rang him up during the afternoon.

"And what," the superintendent asked, as Mr. Jellipot was on the point of putting the same question; "do you make of that?"

"I am puzzled. I was, indeed, so much so that it occupied my thoughts during a short luncheon interval, to the almost entire exclusion of matters of more direct importance to me. I am inclined to the opinion that the man must be approaching an interview at which he intends to demonstrate by production of the cheque both that his transaction is with myself and that it is being done both in a confident and open manner, but that he does not wish any premature or partial indication of what is occurring to come to the knowledge of those who might misread it. It suggests to me that he is engaged in a negotiation of extreme delicacy, unless I should prefer a more menacing word."

"Well, that's what we've thought all along. Inspector Young, who knows a lot more about these matters than most of us do, thinks he's playing poker with one of the hottest gangs of international crooks that infest us here, and New York on the other side. We did warn you that it would have been better to leave the whole thing to us."

"It appeared to me to be a matter for the man himself to decide."

"Well, you've had it your own way."

"I think not," Mr. Jellipot replied in his gentlest and most obstinate tone. "Had he sought my advice, it might have been of an opposite kind."

"Well, you made us let him have his, and that comes to the same thing."

Mr. Jellipot restrained himself from further retort. He had a great respect for the shrewdness of Superintendent Davis. But why were men of far greater ability than himself so inexact in their use of the spoken word? He said amiably: "Well, we'll all hope that it won't get the man into any serious trouble." He put it out of his mind, as requiring nothing further, for the time, either of action or decision from him, until two days later when he heard Mrs. Aide's voice on the telephone again.

It was late evening on this occasion, and the call came through to his private residence, after he had finished a good dinner, such as some wives, and a larger proportion of well-paid housekeepers, can be trusted to serve at the end of a business day, and was succumbing to his solitary indulgence of an after-dinner cigar.

He heard the voice of a frightened woman, and though what she said was more coherent than anything that would have been likely to come from Jane Lovejoy under similar circumstances, it was still less direct and lucid than a most urgent occasion required.

It would also have become evident to anyone overhearing Mr. Jellipot's end of the conversation, which went on from short elucidatory questions to expostulatory protests, that he was being urged to a course of action which he was most unwilling to adopt. Yet adopt it at length he did. For protest changed to reluctant assent. "Then," he said, "I will come at once. I think you will be wise to delay your own—well, it is a point which you must decide for yourself. Yes, I see that. Then I shall arrive about half an hour later than you."

With these words he rang off. There were few things he hated more than being hurried into decisive action before the problem with which he dealt had been subjected to the exhaustive analysis of a normally slow-moving mind. But he recognized the need for prompt action now.

He rang for a taxi to be brought to his door at once. "I am in a hurry," he said. "Send me a man who can drive fast." He reached for his boots.

But having laced them with his accustomed precision, he sat motionless for a long minute before reaching for the telephone again, and asking to be put through to Scotland Yard.

He enquired for Chief Inspector Combridge, and was not surprised to learn that he had left for the day. So, it appeared, had Superintendent Davis. But, if it were a matter of urgency, they could be reached at their own homes."

Mr. Jellipot hesitated upon that. "Is," he asked, "the inspector in who specializes in passport business?"

Inspector Young? Yes, Mr. Jellipot thought that was the name. A moment later Inspector Young was on the wire.

"I want you to listen carefully," Mr. Jellipot said, "or it might be better to have someone listening in who can take down what I say. Very well. You know something about the Rissole case? About the false passport enquiry? So I understood. Then I can come to the point at once.

"Mrs. Aide has just phoned me to say that her husband went to meet an unnamed man this afternoon who was to have given him the name on Rissole's passport in exchange for a payment of ten pounds.

"He took the money in cash, but he had it from me in the form of a crossed cheque. He left the cheque with his wife, and told her that it might be necessary, if he should encounter any difficulty, for it to be produced as evidence of the good faith of the deal. In that event he would send her a letter asking her to take or send the document to him. Half an hour ago she had such a letter, asking her to go with it herself at once."

"And you think she ought to have an escort from us?"

"It's less simple than that. It appears that Aide arranged a code with his wife, so that, if she should receive such a letter, she would know by its wording whether she were to follow it literally or to take other action. By the wording she understood that the man considers himself to be in serious danger, which might become more acute if there were any sign of police interference. He wished her to take the cheque, but to inform me first, leaving further action to my discretion."

"It sounds as though Vestman isn't quite as big a mug as I thought he was when I heard what he was trying to do. Just let us have the address and we'll have a squad there as fast as a car can move."

"I can easily believe that it would be the best way, but I am, unfortunately, pledged to a course of action of a more deliberate character.

"In the first place, there is the possibility that the production of the cheque will be accepted as satisfactory, and the matter be completed without the damage which your intervention might cause."

"It wouldn't be satisfactory to us! What we want is to lay the whole crew by the heels."

"Naturally so. But you cannot be surprised that the Aides look at it from a different angle. Mrs. Aide is already on her way to the place where her husband is detained, and she is anxious that nothing should occur to arouse the hostility of those with whom he is dealing, if they can be satisfied of his good faith."

"She thinks it will end like that? She must be a very sanguine or a very silly woman."

"She is certainly not very wise. But I should not say that she anticipates that. She is apprehensive of a more sinister development. But she wishes to exhaust alternative possibilities.

"In fact, she urged upon me that I should follow her as quickly as possible, as I am proposing to do. She seemed to think that if there should be trouble with which she or Vestman—Aide, as I should say—would be unequal to deal, I might have the ability to compose it."

"You mean you're going into that crowd alone?"

"You think it foolish? I am strongly inclined to the same view. But the fact is that the woman expressed a confidence in my ability which I am unable to share, and she would hear of no other way."

"Well, you should have refused, and just passed it on to us. That's the best thing you can do. We're having the squad got ready now. "

"But the position was less simple than you suppose. The woman was resolved to go herself to her—husband's—aid, but she would not even give me the address unless I undertook to follow her there alone."

"Got a gun?"

"No. It is a weapon which I have neither ability nor inclination to use."

"Well, it's your funeral. What do you want us to do?"

"I am a man of peace," Mr. Jellipot said seriously. "I have no practice with lethal weapons, which the gentlemen whom I am proposing to interview may be more accustomed to use. I must aim to overcome whatever difficulties they may raise on a more rational plane.

"But should I fail, as is, I fear, far more probable than Mrs. Aide's too-confident estimate of my modest powers of persuasion, I shall be pleased to feel that you will be coming upon the scene—shall we say at 11:30 P.M.?"

"That's for you to say. You haven't given me the address yet."

"Which I am unable to do until I have your explicit promise that the interference, or even presence, of the police will not precede the agreed hour, or take place at all if you hear from the Aides or myself that the information has been peacefully obtained."

"Then you must have that. But don't you think 11:30's a bit late for us, if you're going now?"

"Perhaps it is. But I am obliged to remember that prolixity is a feature of my modes of conversation or argument—or perhaps I should call it fault—and I would not risk a premature interruption. Yet perhaps we may safely say 11:15, or even 11:10. The address is 3, Jones's Court, Lower Monkton Street, E.13."

"Very well. We'll be there." Mr. Jellipot excused himself from further conversation, saying that he could hear that his taxi was at the door.

Inspector Young telephoned to Superintendent Davis, who said he would be at the yard in an hour's time. He said that Chief Inspector Combridge should be given an opportunity of being present. Unless they should have heard previously from Mr. Jellipot that the transaction had been peacefully completed, in which event it would be obviously unfair to Henry Vestman to take a course which would be attributed to his treachery, and almost certainly subject him to the future vengeance of the gang, Jones's Court was to be surrounded by the forces of law and order at 11:10, and number three in particular would be ransacked, if necessary, from floor to ceiling.

"And if our watches should happen to be a bit fast," Inspector Young reflected, "I shouldn't say there would be much harm in that."

CHAPTER XXIV.

MR. JELLIPOT HAS TIME FOR THOUGHT

MR. JELLIPOT picked up his umbrella, more from habit than any expectation of requiring it in the interior of a taxi, or on a night of stars, and descended the six steps of his dignified suburban residence to the waiting vehicle.

He was of pacific temperament, and though it is true that he once confused the aim of a deadly weapon by accurate flinging of a most unexpected carafe, he was not encouraged by that solitary incident to suppose that he could perform a physical rescue of Henry Vestman from the hands of the lawless and probably ruthless gang who were detaining him in the repellent neighbourhood of Lower Monkton Street.

He was fastidious, both intellectually and physically, in his dislike of personal violence. It was as illogical as it was vulgar, in its process and its results. He was conscious also that it was a form of conflict in which he was not competent to excel. He could only hope that Bessie Aide's most unwelcome faith in his powers of persuasion and argument might not be disproved by the event. But his greatest hope was that his intervention would not be required. Was it not a reasonable anticipation that on Mrs. Aide's arrival the money would be accepted, the information given, and the criminal companionship quickly disperse, leaving him nothing to do but to turn from a probably unlighted, vacated house?

After that there would be nothing more to do than to ascertain the safety of the Aides, which, by means of a telephone call, would be quickly done.

But Mr. Jellipot, having a particularly logical mind, rebuked himself for allowing it to stray towards that attractive possibility. The taxi was moving rapidly north and east, through streets which Mr. Jellipot did not know, but which were doubtless chosen by the experienced driver for whom he had stipulated as giving him the clearest and therefore most rapid passage. Very soon, if ever, the moment of crisis must arrive. It was that contingency which should entirely engage his thoughts.

Reflecting upon the information which Bessie Aide had given him, he saw little reason to hope that his intervention would not be required. The warning which she had received in that cunningly-coded letter was not likely to be indicative of no more than the baseless fear of a nervous man. Henry Vestman had not impressed him in that way. A cool, criminal, rather surly type, well able to hold his own, and to judge the characters and intentions of those with whom he was dealing now.

It was most probable that his enquiry had alarmed what must be a well-organized and unscrupulous gang, and that they had expressed willingness to supply the required information with no better purpose than to draw him into their power. He might have barely saved his life by revealing that Bessie Aide was in the secret of what he did, and by writing that letter which appeared to enjoin silence upon her while she should be walking into the same trap. Or it must be admitted as an alternative possibility, though one which Mr. Jellipot less confidently entertained, that they might be fairly testing a genuine doubt, and willing to look with impartial eyes upon any evidence which the woman would be able to bring.

Mr. Jellipot was led by these speculations to imagine Henry Vestman most uncomfortably bound and perhaps gagged as he had waited for the woman's arrival. He was influenced to this vision less by the usual exercise of his logical faculty than by the innumerable precedents supplied by novel and screen and stage, from which sources it may be learned that it is an invariable custom of lawless miscreants to bind their victims for a period of hours or even days before inflicting vengeance upon them, although these intervals are almost always utilized to break the bondage by fire or knife, or sheer physical strength if such aids should not be at hand.

Delivering his mind from the hypnotic influence of these representations, Mr. Jellipot considered, with no satisfaction, that if Vestman's captors had coerced him into writing a note which they supposed would bring the woman also into their hands, there would be little apparent reason for keeping him, so to speak, in cold storage until she should arrive. To knock him on the head as soon as the letter was written would surely be the less troublesome method; and on her arrival, if they had decided upon her death, it was mere common sense to conclude that she would be dealt with, promptly in the same manner.

They might have two dead bodies upon their hands when he should arrive, and it was easy to see that he would be a most unwelcome caller under such circumstances. They might conclude that prudence required that he should be served in the same way. Reviewing this contingency in a perturbed but singularly impartial mind, Mr. Jellipot felt that he could hardly blame them for that.

Even though they should be following more conventional methods, Mr. Jellipot felt that his position would be particularly precarious until the arrival of the police, for he had no confidence in his own capacity for rolling towards convenient candles or knives, and severing bonds therewith. He thought it highly likely that knife or candle would not be there.

He might, of course, secrete his penknife where it would be improbable that it would be observed. In his shoe, for instance? He imagined himself with hands and feet securely bound, twisting vainly to break the lace with his teeth to release a weapon which they must then be used to open and operate. It was a vision that had no attraction at all. "Men who do such things," he reflected, "must be remarkable for ingenuity, for perseverance, for suppleness, and for physical strength. Their captors may be reasonably astonished at what they do."

He must hope that both Mr. and Mrs. Aide would have departed, or be still physically intact on his arrival, and it was on his course of action, or rather his choice of words, in this last contingency, that he concentrated his thoughts during the brief interval that remained before he became aware that the taxi had slackened speed, as it moved through a narrow and ill-lit street.

The driver slid back the glass partition to ask: "Know where Jones's Court is, sir?"

Mr. Jellipot admitted ignorance. The street was deserted, though the hour was not late. They moved slowly along what must have been one of the worst rows of slum dwellings that the energies of the L.C.C. had left uncleared. They turned, and crawled halfway down the other side before they came to a narrow entry where a man lounged.

Mr. Jellipot, now at an open window, called to him for information that was civilly and readily given. "Here you are, guv'nor. Up here's the way."

Mr. Jellipot looked at a dark and narrow passage over which a combination of sight and imagination, aided by a street lamp at no great distance, enabled him to read the name of the place he sought.

"Shall I wait, sir?" the driver asked. The place certainly did not appear to be one at which any gentleman would wish to pay a long call at that hour.

Mr. Jellipot said: "Yes, I don't suppose I shall be many minutes." He had an impulse to add: "And if I'm more than that you'd better get a call through to Scotland Yard, and tell them to hurry up." But a habit of restraining speech until it could be endorsed by a considered judgment gave him time to observe that the man of whom he had enquired now stood close enough to overhear anything he might say. His tone had been civil enough, but his face, better seen as he came forward, looked to be that of one who would most naturally talk in a more truculent way. Mr. Jellipot's caution confined itself to withdrawing his hand from a pocket into which he had already delved for the fare. If the driver were unpaid, he would be the more sure to remain. He must leave it at that.

The driver sat for about half an hour after Mr. Jellipot disappeared down that dark entry, followed by the man who had been lounging at its mouth. At the end of that time, the man appeared again. "It's no use waiting there, mate," he said, in what was meant to be a friendly voice, "unless you've got nothing better to do. The gent's been gone ten minutes now."

"I reckon you're wrong there. I should have seen him come out."

"So you might if he'd come this way. But he went out into Raglan Street. You might catch him somewhere round there, if you move quick."

"You mean there's a way out of this court to another street?"

The man laughed shortly. "That there is. Never been bilked that way before?"

"Yes. But not this time. Why didn't you tell the gentleman, if you saw him going the wrong way?"

"How was I to tell that he didn't know what he was after? It weren't no business of mine. And I'd say he did. But I didn't like to see you sitting here. You might say thanks to a pal for a straight tip."

The driver said nothing more, good or bad. He drove round into Raglan Street, where enquiry proved the truth of the man's assertion that there was another exit from Jones's Court. He was in no fear of losing his fare, for he knew Mr. Jellipot, whom he had driven more than once before. But the thing looked a bit queer. Queer, but not impossible. If Mr. Jellipot had no knowledge of there being more than one exit, he might easily have made the mistake. One passage may look very like another in the dusk of an ill-lit court.

The driver's doubt was enough to cause him to leave his vehicle, and go up the Raglan Street passage himself. He stumbled in a narrow ill-paved yard surrounded by a dozen houses, in two or three of which faint lights showed behind tattered blinds. But he did not even know to which of them Mr Jellipot had gone. And if the solicitor had made that mistake, and emerged on an empty street, what would he conclude but that he had become tired of waiting and driven off? He drove back to the garage from which he came, reported the incident, and had the fare booked. He went out on another job.

CHAPTER XXV.

Mr. Jellipot Breaks a Cup

As Mr. Jellipot went up the entry he looked at his watch, which had a luminous dial. It was seven minutes to ten. That gave him almost an hour before it would be too late to prevent the coming of the police, if all should go well. It should, he considered, be ample time. Or, if not? Then it would be a full hour and a quarter before he could expect them to arrive. It might be longer than he would wish!

But Mr. Jellipot was a man of deliberation, both in physical and mental processes. He did not like to be rushed, though he had shown more than once that he could think or act with promptitude when occasion called. At this moment he would have been very unlikely to shorten the time at his disposal, had the opportunity of decision been presented to him anew.

The court was dark. There was a faint light in a ground-floor window of a house on the further side: another in a nearer bedroom. But how was he to find number three, with no better light? He went forward treading uneven bricks, and most conscious of a bad smell. His foot sank slightly in a shallow gutter which ran down to a central drain.

He struck a match, and examined one of the doors. It had a half-obliterated figure still visible on its time-worn paint. Number three. Or else eight. A second match decided the doubt. Certainly eight. He would count round from that point, and take a fifty-fifty chance of moving in the right direction.

Having done this, he struck another match, and examined a door the battered surface of which showed no number at all. He knocked, and an echo of emptiness was the only response he got. He thought: "Where there is light there will be life. I was foolish not to enquire at once."

He crossed to the house which showed a ground-floor light through its tattered blind. When he knocked, the door opened at once. A huge form confronted him, almost blocking sight of an untidy living room, in which a woman sat sewing, and a baby sprawled on a fireside rug.

"Can you kindly direct me to number three?" Mr. Jellipot asked politely. "The light is unfortunately insufficient to—"

The giant, without answering him directly, turned his head inward: "Gert, which is number three?"

Mr. Jellipot had a side view of the red, good-humoured face of a Covent Garden porter, who might have lived in a better place had he drank less.

Gert answered readily, though in the dull voice of one whom ill-health or overwork made incurious of surrounding things. "Number three? That'll be the Timsons. Last house on the other side."

The man turned back to the door. "You want Timsons?" he asked.

"Yes," Mr. Jellipot answered with a noncommittal note in his voice which did not suggest a close acquaintance with any family of that name, "I suppose I do. I want number three."

"Well, that's who lives there. Queer bunch, aren't they, Gert?" The woman answered as listlessly as before: "They just keep to themselves. They're not often there. They're away at sea more times than not."

Mr. Jellipot felt assured, as he heard this, that it was the house he sought. After being directed to it with more particularity, he expressed his gratitude and took his way across the court. He was aware that the door he had left remained open, and that the man was still gazing after him. He did not mind that. It gave him a feeling that friendly human interest and possible support were not far away. But the door closed as he approached that which he sought, and the silent darkness was around him again.

He had a belated thought that he might have saved himself a good deal of trouble had he asked the man who had been lounging at the entrance of the court to guide him to number three. But he had seen nothing of him from the moment when he had entered the passage and he was one whom he had not liked—and he might not have known—and, anyhow, he was here now. He raised his umbrella in a resolute hand and knocked loudly upon the door. Until that moment he had heard no sign from a house which showed no light, and that did not appear large enough to be occupied without some outward evidence, but in response to the sharp rap he gave he heard an inner door open. Voices became audible. A faint light showed through a cracked and ill-fitting door, and a woman's step came down the passage.

She was the first to speak as she opened the door. "Mr. Jellipot, I expect?" she said pleasantly. "Please come in."

There was a tall old-fashioned hat-stand in the narrow hall, at which she invited him to deposit hat and umbrella, after which she led the way to the back room from which she had come.

Mr. Jellipot looked upon a table spread with a white cloth and an ample meal. Several people, including Mr. and Mrs. Aide, were in the room. He blinked upon a scene different from anything he had been expecting to meet.

The woman who had let him in was speaking again. She appeared elderly, but not showing any weakness of age. She was short and slim. Quick in her movements, with bright, alert, restless eyes. She had an abundance of hair, silvery white. Her voice was very soft, like a soothing purr. "We hoped," she said, "that you'd join us as you've come so far. It's a kindness that we appreciate very much, though it wasn't really necessary, Mrs. Aide having cleared everything up that we need to know. It's not exactly dinner, it's more like what we call high tea in Yorkshire. Just a slice of cold ham, and some hot cakes and a cup of good tea."

Mr. Jellipot answered: "It's very kind of you, but I had dinner just before I came out. I'm afraid I couldn't eat anything more now. I'm an abstemious man. But it's very kind of you to have considered me, all the same. You are from Yorkshire, madam?"

He spoke almost randomly, seeking delay to get the bearings of this unexpected reception, and decide what it could mean.

"No, I'm not Yorkshire," the woman answered, "but I've got a married sister living there, and I visit her once a year, or more often than that. Mrs. Orton's my name. I dare say you've heard of us from Mr. Aide."

"Mr. Aide has been most discreet. He mentioned no names at all."

"So he said, but we're all friends here now. I'm only sorry Mr. Orton had to go earlier. He'd have been so pleased to meet you. There's no profession he admires more than the law. Though I suppose you'd say we don't show much respect for it by some of the things we do."

"I'm afraid I couldn't answer that, madam—Mrs. Orton I should say. But it's no business of mine," Mr. Jellipot answered cautiously, more bewildered than before by this easy frankness of confession, in a tone that made law-breaking a mere tea-party affair. He was listening to the woman with half his mind, and with the other studying the room and its occupants. These latter she now introduced in an informal manner, but with the same frankness as before.

"My nephew, Charles—our artist, Mr. Poynter—my daughter. Sissie—Mr. and Mrs. Aide you already know. Even if you've had dinner, Mr. Jellipot, a cup of tea's always welcome. I feel sure you won't refuse to join us in that."

"Yes, a cup of tea's always welcome, Mr. Jellipot." The echoed words came from Vestman, rather awkwardly spoken, but Mr. Jellipot judged that he was being asked, with whatever object, to remain, as he had already decided to do.

The domestic scene might disprove—might even render ridiculous—the lurid imagination which he had indulged in the last hour, but it did not supply the explanation he wished to have. Certainly he would stay, for half an hour if not more, and there would still be time to stop the police from making a raid which might be successful in capturing criminals—the woman's curious frankness seemed to give an affirmative answer to that—but it had an aspect of treachery which he did not like, if Vestman's fears had been groundless, and the vendors of illicit passports were making a straightforward deal with him.

Seated by a cheerful fire, in an old but very comfortable armchair, while the rest of the little party took chairs at the loaded table, Mr. Jellipot considered the position.

He looked round the room. The furniture was good enough, but of a style suitable for the best room of such a dwelling as that to which it belonged. He observed that the door had a felt surround. Doubtless that was why there had been no sign of light from the room when it was closed. But that might not be its object. It might be a device to keep out draughts, such as the ill-fitting doors of these old houses might reasonably require. The window was not shuttered. It lacked even a drawn blind. It might, of course, look out on no more than a blank wall, as, in fact, it did.

Mr. Jellipot could not know that, but he saw that such speculations wasted his time. These people were confessedly of criminal habits, and there must be occasions when they would prefer to be unobserved. There was no significance whatever in that.

He supposed that if Combridge had been in his place he would already have observed and inferred about ten times more than he, himself, would ever be likely to do. Still, he must do his best.

There was little else of singularity about the room, unless it were that it was lit with a paraffin table-lamp. It was a good lamp, giving plenty of light, but Mr. Jellipot remembered that there had been electric lighting at the first house at which he had called. Why not here? Doubtless because they did not want meter inspectors intruding with an official right. That was obvious too. He must do better than this.

Was it not the real and only puzzle that Vestman should have been so seriously alarmed? The house did not appear to be difficult to leave. The people were not very formidable for one of Vestman's physique. Certainly Mrs. Orton was not. Nor was Sissie a rather squat young woman, with a sullen dull face. Nor was Poynter, the "artist," a tall, very thin, sallow-faced man, with an ugly scar on his forehead. He had very long, sensitive, well-kept hands. A long, very thin nose. He gave an effect of length without breadth. Mr. Jellipot could easily believe that he was excellent at the forging of passports, or documents of more direct monetary value. Probably one whom the police would be glad to have. But he did not appear to be of a combative kind.

Charles, Mrs. Orton's nephew, was of a different pattern. A broad-shouldered man. Thick-necked, thick-lipped, with heavy jaws, and small, cunning, pig-like eyes. He had the look of one who went the way of the sea.

But it must not be forgotten that there had been another there. Mr. Orton, who had gone, and who might be more formidable than any he had left. Mr. Jellipot saw that his departure might be of decisive significance. There might have been angry scenes here, or in an upper room, in the earlier day. Suspicion. Threats. Those who live by such means must be in continual dread of betrayal to the police, and their only security must come from fear of their lawless vengeance. Threats of murder, if not murder itself, must be the almost inevitable outcome of such organized activities, whenever they lost confidence in any who were in the secrets of what they did.

If they thought that Vestman was in the pay of the police, and were seeking to trap them into supplying evidence for their own undoing, he might have passed through an unpleasant ordeal a few hours ago. But now it appeared that they had accepted his assurances, to the point not merely of believing that it was only on behalf of himself that the enquiry had been made, but that he—Mr. Jellipot—was worthy of equal trust. Mr. Jellipot, thinking thus, was conscious of a momentary resentment that he should have been given so dubious a confidence. Was he so regarded in criminal circles because he had once or twice been led by malicious circumstance to defend those who had been accused of capital crimes? How precarious human reputation is, how unfair deductions can be!

There was another inmate of the house, to whom Mr. Jellipot was not introduced—a young woman who served at the table, bringing in plates of hot cakes and other dishes, for the variety of the meal went beyond the cold ham of which Mrs. Orton had spoken.

Mr. Jellipot, watching her, was puzzled as to the girl's status. She did a servant's tasks, but did not speak to Mrs. Orton as a mistress would be addressed. She was neatly clad and pretty in a cheap way, but Mr. Jellipot, though disinclined to uncharitable judgments, classified her as sharp-witted, spiteful, and sly. Well, what did he expect? Saintly characters here? There appeared at least to be good humour and good spirits to enliven the meal. The little party seemed to have accepted the Aides without reservation now, nor did they allow his own quiet presence to check their mirth, or the freedom of what they said.

Mr. Jellipot watched and thought. He observed Mrs. Orton whisper briefly to the waiting girl, who went out. It might be no more than a direction of service, of no importance, but Mr. Jellipot's hearing was good. He thought that, when she left the room a moment after, it was not the kitchen but the front door to which she went. Actually, she had a few words with a lurking man which resulted in the conversation with the waiting taxi driver which has been told already.

Mr. Jellipot could not guess this. The incident, trivial in itself, might have no significance. The girl had not been more than three minutes away. When she came back, she said quite openly to Mrs. Orton: "That's all right. Shall I use the brown tea-pot?"

The promised tea had not yet been brought in. The little company drank water, an example for many of more law-respecting habits. Mrs. Orton glanced round, as though counting her guests. "Yes," she said, "but we shall need more than that. You'd better make it in the white one as well."

A few minutes later the two pots came in. Mr. Jellipot must come to the table now. Chairs were pushed closer to make room for him at Mrs. Orton's left hand. It was now twenty minutes to eleven. Mr. Jellipot supposed that there would still be time to stop the police. Just time. Perhaps still time in five minutes. Should he excuse himself? Not just yet. But he saw that he ran a risk which perhaps, in fairness to Mr. and Mrs. Aide, he ought not to do: risk that he would be too late to stop them, and that he would have acted contrary to the wishes and interests of those to whom he conceived that his first duty lay. But the seconds passed, and he did not move.

Mrs. Orton began to fill the seven cups that were arrayed before her. She honoured Mr. Jellipot with her first attention. "Sugar. Mr. Jellipot?"

"Yes. Two lumps, please."

Mrs. Orton approved. She said she could not understand anyone not preferring sugar in tea. It took off the bitter taste. "Don't you think so, Mrs. Aide?"

It appeared that Mrs. Aide did. There were to be two lumps for her. And perhaps Mr. Aide had the same taste? Well, more or less. It was one lump for him. The Aides were served as this conversation went on.

Mr. Jellipot was still in a puzzled doubt. He was sipping his tea now, his cup raised to his lips in one hand, the saucer closely beneath it in the other, in an attitude which cannot be recommended for imitation. He observed that passport forgers appeared to like their tea black and strong. But there was nothing illegal in that.

Mrs. Orton was now pouring out for her other guests. Mr. Jellipot glanced round the table. Mrs. Orton, as we know, was nearest to him on the right. The girl, Sissie, sat on his left hand. It must be one or other, and another second would be too late. He preferred Mrs. Orton. He brought cup and saucer down with smashing force on the woman's head.

CHAPTER XXVI.

The Consequences of Breaking China

THE woman sank in her chair, actually stunned by the blow, though its force had been partly broken by the wig which now slipped sideways upon her head, exposing a stubble of closely-cropped, dull-red hair, and that she was fifteen years younger than she had looked a moment before. Broken china scattered around her. Tea dripped down her face and shoulders.

Mr. Jellipot glanced round the startled table. "It was," he remarked in his mildest and most casual voice, "an unpleasant necessity, the reason for which some of you may appreciate; in which case you convict yourselves. Stop him, Vestman."

The last words were sharply spoken, for Charles, reacting more quickly to the situation than his companions, had risen, an oath on his lips, and a table-knife in his hand. Vestman was almost as quick to rise, and the next moment the two were struggling upon the ground, impeded by the legs of a fallen chair.

Mr. Jellipot looked at Poynter, who had also risen, in a state of obvious indecision.

"I don't see," he began in a voice of ineffectual protest.

"If you are a wise man," Mr. Jellipot interrupted, fixing him with a steady glance, "you won't interfere in this at all. You won't understand what has occurred, or why two women, if no others, will go to jail for the next fifteen years."

"No. I don't understand. I don't understand at all."

"Then you will do well to stand back, and leave it to those who do."

Mr. Jellipot saw that the position was well in hand, if this man would leave it alone. He would not ask him for more than that.

Mrs. Aide had gone to her husband's assistance with kicks that were quick and hard, and with no mercy in where they fell. The knife had dropped or been wrenched from the seaman's hand. There was no doubt of who would be victors there.

Sissie alone remained at the table still, adding no more than noise to the scene. She sat staring at her senseless parent, and howled on a high note.

The girl who had served the tea ran into the room, hearing the noise made by the screaming and the men who fought on the floor. Mr. Jellipot recognized that it was his duty to deal with her, and a less pleasant one may not have been his during nearly thirty years of legal practice.

The girl's eyes fell on her mistress first, and she ran to her with a sharp cry. As she did so, Mr. Jellipot grasped her arms from behind. "I arrest you," he said, "for attempted murder. You will be well advised—" The sentence remained incomplete, for he became busy in other ways.

Screaming foul curses, the girl struggled, twisted and fought. She kicked backward with vicious heels. Her teeth met in his wrist.

The scene roused the howling Sissie like an electric shock. She sprang from her chair. Was he to have two fighting females upon him at once? It was no more than an instant's fear. "It's all your doing, you dirty cat! And look what you've done now!" Sissie screamed. She struck the face of the struggling girl with heavy shapeless hands. Mr. Jellipot found it necessary to solicit the aid of the irresolute Poynter to save his captive from the savagery of the younger girl.

Even at this moment of unusual activity Mr. Jellipot had sufficient detachment of mind to reflect on the vanity of all forecasts of the vagaries of human experience. He had imagined himself ignominiously bound with ropes that he could not break, and here he was with a most urgent occasion for binding others, and his eyes searched the room in vain for any suitable coil.

He could not hold indefinitely a girl who was little weaker than he, and whose struggles were only sullenly suspended lest Sissie's nails should be exercised on her face, which anyone whose arms are held from behind would prefer to avoid. Vestman could not sit on Charles's head forever, even with the competent feminine assistance that had enabled him to subdue his opponent.

The neutral Poynter might walk out of the room at any moment, and Mr. Jellipot felt sure that the police would prefer to include him in their collection. He could scarcely ask him to go to obtain ropes with which to bind those who had been his friends of the last hour. And Mrs. Orton showed signs of returning consciousness, which Mr. Jellipot regarded as his most serious difficulty, for he suspected that she had brains, of which he had seen little sign in that room since hers had been put out of action. But his dilemma ended abruptly with the sound of a loud knocking at the street door, which changed next moment to that of a breaking lock.

An inspector entered the room whom he did not know, and looked round with experienced eyes. "You look," he said, "as though you could do with some handcuffs here. Sergeant, take that young woman off Mr. Jellipot's hands. Your wrist's bleeding, sir. rather badly."

But Mr. Jellipot had matters on his mind of more importance than a bitten wrist. His eyes went to a clock on the mantelpiece that ticked indifferently its record of time in the disordered room. It was just five past eleven.

"If," he said, "you are Inspector Young, I must point out that you are here before the agreed time, which might have put me in a very awkward position—very awkward indeed."

"Sorry, sir, but I only obeyed orders. You must talk to the superintendent about that."

Inspector Young had actually done nothing more than put a most reliable clock eight minutes fast in Superintendent Davis's room.

CHAPTER XXVII.

A DAMNING FACT

SUPERINTENDENT Davis looked round the room. "Glad to see you, Poynter," he said, in a voice which had no lack of sincerity. "We didn't know you were in with this gang. You needn't handcuff *him*, Sergeant, he'll come quietly enough."

"Mr. Jellipot," the man answered, in a shaking voice, "will tell you that I've done nothing wrong. I've been helping him all I could."

"That so, Mr. Jellipot?"

"Without endorsing in its entirety the comprehensive certification which Mr. Poynter claims from me, either in respect of his usual integrity or his activities during the past ten minutes, I am disposed to say that there is some basis—or perhaps percentage would be a better word—some percentage of truth in his contention that he should not be too closely identified with his present companions, or the crime with which they must now be charged, until further enquiry has been made, and he has been heard in his own defence, if there should be anything he may wish to say." The superintendent turned his eyes to the woman who had now recovered her senses sufficiently to be aware of the handcuffs upon her wrists. He pulled off the slanting wig.

"Glad to see you too, Liza. Wanting you for the last three years has given me the worst headache I ever had. It's queer how much difference a wig can make." He put the crown of silver-grey hair back on the head of the silent woman for a moment to survey its effect, and perhaps to consider how far his subordinates should be excused for their failure to see through the disguise.

The look the woman gave him as he pulled it off and handed it to one of his attendant officers with the remark, "Take care of that. I expect the lawyers'll call it Exhibit A," was an ugly mixture of hate and fear, but she only said in her softest voice: "I don't understand in the least what this means, or what I'm supposed to have done, but Mr. Jellipot's a witness that I've said nothing, and I don't intend to till I've got a good lawyer present."

"You'll need a good one, if Mr. Jellipot starts calling you names," the superintendent replied in his good-humoured voice. "But don't say anything you don't want. You'll find that's all right with us."

He looked round at the other occupants of the room, and his looks of satisfaction lessened. "Young," he said, "you wouldn't call it a full catch?"

"No, sir. It wasn't these women, it was Orton we hoped to get."

"Anything upstairs?"

"Combridge has gone up there, sir. I should say there's something interesting by the time he's been. But we're not likely to find Orton there."

"No. You say you want everything on the table left just as it is, Mr. Jellipot? So it shall be, till we get the photographers here. And nothing touched in the kitchen? Sergeant Boulton will see to that."

As he spoke, Inspector Combridge entered the room. "Two upper floors," he said, "and two rooms on each. Front rooms vacant. Back attic a bedroom, that doesn't look as though it's much used. The lower bedroom's the interesting place. They seem to have used this house as a hiding-hole which no one would be likely to find, even if they should get run in."

"I wonder in whose name it was rented," Superintendent Davis said.

"We know that, sir," Inspector Young answered. "I got the agent for these properties on the phone at his private address while I was waiting for you to come. It was sold to a man named Charles Timson about two years ago—the man that they're putting into the van now, more likely than not."

"Well, we'd better be getting off. Even policemen like to get some sleep now and then. There's nothing here that won't keep till morning. But if you can come back with us, Mr. Jellipot, we should be glad to have your account of what's been happening here, and what you mean by attempted murder, though I know you're not one to make such an accusation without knowing what you're about."

"As a matter of fact," Mr. Jellipot replied cautiously, "the exigency of the moment obliged me to assume more than I can accurately be said to know, but I will assert with some confidence that the cups of tea which still lie before the place where Mr. and Mrs. Aide sat, together with the white pot from which they were poured, will give you all the evidence you require, although the theoretic possibilities that they may contain nothing more detrimental than a strong narcotic or even be entirely innocuous can only be eliminated by the chemical tests which will doubtless be tried upon them."

Superintendent Davis picked up Mrs. Aide's cup. He smelt it, and then ventured to test its taste with a cautious tongue. "Couldn't say," he admitted; "but I expect you've made a good guess. Mrs. Orton, if that's her proper name now, was acquitted on a poisoning charge about twelve years ago, for no better reason than that the jury liked her voice and her red hair. No one could have been quite as innocent as she looked in the box. She's been about everything that a woman shouldn't since then. But we'll get along now, if you don't mind, and have these beauties properly charged."

But Mr. Jellipot did not move. "We must not," he said, "forget the purpose which brought us here." He turned to Vestman, who was now seated beside the fire, while his companion, who had suffered less physical damage in their common victory, ministered to the cuts and bruises he had sustained. "I hope you were successful in obtaining the information for which you came."

"Yes. They gave me that, if it's the right dope, and I'd say it is. They didn't seem to mind what they told me, or what they showed. It was that, or them trying to find out all the time if anyone knew I'd come, that made me sure they were up to no good, and write to Bessie the way I did. But it's Orton you ought to get. He's a slimy devil. He never meant me to get out of here alive from the minute I entered the door. He was here up to about two hours ago, when I suppose he thought he'd left everything fixed, when he heard you were to come."

"I've no doubt the police will be equal to dealing with him. You say they gave you the information for which you came?"

"Yes. The name was Antonio Gardini. They were American papers. Born in Hoboken. Italian father. That's what they were made to say."

Superintendent Davis observed that Mr. Jellipot was not lightly to be turned from that which he had undertaken to do. He admitted candidly to his own mind that the passport expedients of Tony Rissole had ceased to interest him, in the excitement of this far more important capture. He saw that Mr. Jellipot was making a careful note of the particulars he had heard. Well, he should be sufficient for that! Superintendent Davis's eyes fell upon Poynter, who was still in the room, in a state of quasi-liberty, neither arrested nor free. "Like to do something for us?" he asked, looking hard into the man's apprehensive eyes.

"Yes, sir. Anything that I can."

138

"Combridge, is there a phone on the premises?"

"There's one in the back room on the first floor."

"Then you'd better take Poynter upstairs. He can ring up Orton, and say something that'll bring him here."

Mr. Poynter looked more frightened than before. "I couldn't possibly do that. I shouldn't know what to say."

"You haven't said that you don't know his phone number, which means you do, and that's the only good excuse you could have made. You won't tell me that you can't make up a good lie, with ten years' freedom at stake, which is about what you've got to think of. It's helping us now, and when you get put in the box that'll bring you through, if anything will."

"I don't mind doing what I can," the man said eagerly. "But not this. And I don't see why I need. You could arrest him another way."

"That's for us to decide. But I'll tell you straight. We can't arrest him because *we don't know who he is*. We want you to get him here with any tale that you like to tell, and you'll have done something we shan't forget. You needn't be funky for anything he can do to you. He won't have a chance of that for a long time to come. "

The man made no further protest. He followed Inspector Combridge out of the room.

The arrest of Orton might be important to the police, but it was less so to Mr. Jellipot, though he saw that Superintendent Davis's methods raised questions of ethical probity which it might be interesting to consider in quieter hours. He said: "Well, that means you'll be staying here for a time. It ought to give me time to drive round to my office before—or, perhaps, you won't mind if I don't come to the Yard at all till tomorrow morning. I really have had a tiring day."

Superintendent Davis made no demur. He had sufficient information now on which to detain his prisoners till the next day, and he had no objection to getting as much sleep himself as might still be possible after the unknown Orton had been lured into his hands by a voice he knew.

Mr. Jellipot, late though it was, drove down to his office to examine the list of passengers with which he had been supplied.

As he looked down it, the last doubt of the guilt of Tony Rissole passed from his mind. Antonio Gardini was recorded to have sailed for New York from London in the *American Merchant* on Saturday, February 21st. There could be few facts of circumstantial evidence more conclusive than that.

CHAPTER XXVIII.

MR. JELLIPOT GIVES HIS REASONS

IT was at eleven o'clock on the following morning that Mr. Jellipot sat in Superintendent Davis's unusually crowded office, and explained how he had deduced and frustrated the crime of which he would have been one of the triple victims. He spoke to an assembly of prominent officers of the C.I.D., who were elated by the success of one of the most important captures of recent years, and disposed to congratulate both themselves and him. For they had found evidences in the unsuspected hiding-place of that upper room in Jones's Court of other things than the forging of passports, and Orton had walked into the trap; and had proved to be a criminal of international importance whose identity might otherwise have remained unguessed. With Poynter as King's Evidence they had the prospect of a successful prosecution, with added reputation to themselves which they had, in fact, done singularly little to earn. The Rissole murder was a comparatively trivial matter, of which they thought scarcely at all.

"It was while they were at the table, talking, and taking little notice of me," Mr. Jellipot began, "that I had leisure to think, and the idea came to my mind.

"The frank talk that was addressed to me, and more which I overheard at the table, was evidently intended to make us feel that we were trusted, but I formed the opinion that it was overdone.

"I can certainly claim no credit for exceptional acumen in arriving at that conclusion, which Vestman had previously formed on much inferior data, for they might more naturally have regarded him—a man of past criminal associations, and who had recommended a customer for their illicit wares—as one of themselves than they could have placed me in that category, even had I been acting for him in a manner which would have been a degradation of my professional honour, as they might possibly have been led to believe.

"I concluded that whatever action they had resolved to take had been deferred only sufficiently to get me into their power, when, as they had been led to believe, there would be no one left alive who would be aware that we had gone to that secret den.

"I considered, therefore, that I was in acute physical danger, and a natural timidity of disposition rendered it difficult for me to maintain the casual aspect which was essential—or appeared to me to be so—if I were to have the uninterrupted leisure which the position so clearly demanded, to enable me to analyse and frustrate their purpose.

"I confess that for some minutes I was completely baffled. It appeared to me that I could do nothing until they should show their hands, when it might be too late to avoid the fate which they had designed. While we sat there, a messenger—such as the man who had shown me the entrance to the court—might be summoning those whom we should have no power to resist.

"Thinking thus, I was inclined to challenge the position by insisting on an immediate departure, and I should probable have taken this course, with whatever consequence, had I not remembered that you would so soon be approaching to our relief. To endeavour to pass the interval in apparent amity seemed the less perilous alternative.

"But I was still intrigued in mind as to what their plan for our extinction would be most likely to be. A threefold murder of those who are not asleep or entirely devoid of suspicion could not be accomplished without danger of outcry, or not so, at least, by most of the methods which memory or imagination enabled me to marshal in the limited time that I had available. And almost all methods of violence, other than suffocation, have the common feature that they involve the shedding of blood, the traces of which are notoriously difficult to remove.

"How, I asked, should I myself proceed, if my dilemma and moral code were akin to theirs? To this question there was an instant and obvious answer. I should reject violence for reasons I have already stated, and others equally cogent which I need not enumerate, as a clumsy and most dangerous method. Poison would be my almost certain choice. And as I thought this, I saw that the stage was set for such an event. The meal—and surely one such was not often served in that secret resort—had been kept back till I should arrive. And when I had come, they had pressed me to take tea with them, but accepted readily my excuse that I should not eat.

"I heard the instructions for tea to be served in a second pot without surprise, but as making an approximate certainty of that which had been no more than theoretic suspicion before. Until its arrival, I contented myself with watching that no dish was pressed upon my two companions in danger of which others did not partake, but there was no sign of that—nor any great probability while I sat apart.

"When the two pots were brought in, I was not surprised that we were served as we were, but even that might have been no more than a natural courtesy to invited guests. Yet the conversation concerning the bitterness of tea, and the need for sugar, which prepared us in advance for any flavour we might otherwise have observed, was fresh weight in a scale that already sank, and I noticed that Mrs. Orton selected the largest lumps of sugar in the bowl for Mrs. Aide and myself, and dropped two—one before and one after pouring out—into that of Vestman, though she bad been told that one was what he preferred.

"I have a strong antipathy to taking any decisive action without full warrant for what I do, but at that moment I resolved that it Mrs. Orton's hand went to the other pot to fill the next cup—the white one evidently not having been exhausted of its contents—I would act at once on the assumption that we had been handed poison to drink.

"I had by that time tasted my own tea, though taking little more than would wet the tongue, but even so I had been aware of a bitterness which I felt sure to be something more than the fancy of a suspicious man.

"When I saw the second teapot taken up for the next cup, there was no further moment to lose, for Mrs. Aide was in the act of raising her own cup for what might have been a fatal draught.

"It was too late for words to avail. It had become necessary to take some instantaneous action of so startling a nature as would arrest the cup which was within an inch of her lips, as I broke my own over the poisoner's head.

"Some sudden, violent, arresting action, I was, as I have said, obliged to take, and I could think of no better choice than to eliminate one who was within my reach, and whom I regarded as the most dangerous of our enemies. Physical strength she might lack, but the brains were hers, and they are much harder to overcome. As it was, those who were conscious of what they did acted with no more intelligence than does a fowl that runs round having lost its head."

"You reckoned," Inspector Combridge asked curiously, "that you'd knock the old girl out?"

"I had neither experience," Mr. Jellipot replied, "of the effect of breaking a cup on a woman's head, nor time to arrive at a considered opinion of a reliable kind. I could only strike with all the strength that I could exert. But I certainly aimed at that which I might have accomplished even more thoroughly had it not been for that protecting wig, the existence of which I had seen no cause to suspect. "

"Well, we all wish you could have been one of us," Superintendent Davis concluded generously. "It was good work, and probably saved Mrs. Aide's life, if not Vestman's—Mr. Aide's we must try to remember to say—as well. Not to speak of your own risk, if you'd been a bit simpler than you were. But there's one thing I ought to tell you. Mr. Aide won't have to use that cheque you gave him. We've got the notes that he paid Orton, and we're handing them back to him."

Mr. Jellipot looked troubled. "I'm not sure that you ought to do that. There seems to be no doubt that he got the information for which he paid. I've checked on it, and a man with the passport in question sailed from here on the *American Merchant* on Saturday, February the 21st last."

"On Saturday, February 21st," the superintendent echoed, his thoughts less on the date than on what he considered to be Mr. Jellipot's fantastic scruple. Yet at the back of his mind a puzzled doubt stirred, and became still as Mr. Jellipot answered his spoken word.

"Yes. I think you may take it as final and conclusive evidence of Tony Rissole's guilt. He committed the murder, and left the country at once in an assumed name, which he otherwise had no reason to do."

Superintendent Davis accepted this conclusion—particularly emphatic as coming from one of Mr. Jellipot's habit of careful words—and proceeded to discuss the ethics of buying information on an illegal matter from those who intend your death, and then forcibly repossessing yourself of the money paid; on which he and Mr. Jellipot did not agree.

But he did not allow himself to neglect the Rissole case because a more dramatic capture had now been made. It was during the same afternoon that he said: "Combridge, I've just learnt that the *American Merchant* is in dock now. You'd better see if the same steward who waited on Tony Rissole is still on the staff. I expect he will be; there's not overmuch shifting about in those U.S.L. boats.

"Get his description of Rissole, if you can. If he's sure he could identify him, it may be necessary to have him here when the case comes on."

Inspector Combridge said that he would go down to the docks at once. It might be no more than routine now, but it was no less imperative if the case against an obvious murderer were to be built up to the degree of proof which the law requires.

CHAPTER XXIX.

"IT ISN'T POSSIBLE"

CHIEF INSPECTOR COMBRIDGE had some causes to feel content, both with himself and the world around him. The public blunder of arresting Edwin Lovejoy for a crime of which he was entirely innocent had been avoided—how narrowly only he and his colleagues would ever know—and the cautious, patient, persistent methods which he was accustomed to employ were about to be justified once more by the conviction of the actual criminal, who was already in safe custody, and due to be landed at Southampton during the nest forty-eight hours.

But, in fact, he had ceased to care much about the Rissole case, now that its exasperating uncertainty was at an end. His mind was on the more dramatic and far more important arrests of the Orton gang, for which his department (which often did good work for which it got little praise) was receiving much public commendation, where it might more logically have been criticized for not having proved equal to dealing with a widespread criminal organization until it had been, as it were, led to the prey.

But though he felt a lessened interest in the Rissole case, and no further anxiety whatever, he did not therefore neglect the work which was still necessary before it could be placed in legal hands as a finished thing with which it had become their business to deal.

He went beyond the letter of Superintendent Davis's instructions by first visiting the offices of the United States Lines, and there formally confirming the fact that a man having a passport in the name of Antonio Gardini had actually sailed on the *American Merchant* on Saturday, February 21st.

He said it might be necessary for a clerk to attend the trial to give evidence on that point, and was assured that this would be arranged.

"We shall want," he said, "either from someone here, or someone who was aboard the ship, evidence of the exact hour of sailing. The man's wanted for the Rissole murder. We've no doubt he was the same one that we're bringing back from New York now.

"We know the murder was committed late in the afternoon, or perhaps early in the evening would be a more exact way of putting it. We shall have to prove that he'd have had time to get on to the boat after that."

"Well, if that's what he really did, there shouldn't be much trouble in proving that it was not impossible," the traffic superintendent to whom he spoke replied, with reason in what he said. "But I shouldn't think you'll find there's any difficulty on that point. Those boats don't usually sail till about midnight: anyway, I can tell you in two minutes."

He consulted a table of the Thames tides, and said: "It wouldn't have cast off till 12:30 A.M., or a few minutes after that. Anyone could have got aboard up to 12:15, though they're expected earlier."

"And how long would it take to get down to the dock from the West End?"

"It's a slow journey most ways of doing it, but anyone in a hurry can get there by taxi well under the hour, especially when it's late, and there's not much traffic on the streets."

Inspector Combridge considered this information sufficiently satisfactory, and he proceeded to verify it by driving down to the King George V Dock, where the *American Merchant* lay, taking in cargo, as it was her habit to do for four or five days before turning round for her journey home. He had been given a pass to the vessel, the name of the cabin steward, Eric Fenner, who had waited on Antonio Gardini, and the information that the man, being a native of New York, and having his home and family there, would probably economize by remaining on the vessel while in harbour, as he was permitted, though not obliged, to do.

At the cost of an hour's waiting, Inspector Combridge obtained an interview with the man he sought. A small man, with hair so blond as to be almost white, and an honest face, Fenner combined the characteristics of Irish father and Swedish mother with the alert vitality of the city that gave him birth. He appeared likely to prove an excellent witness, and his evidence was all that could be desired. Shown a photograph of Tony Rissole, he recognized it instantly as that of the Antonio Gardini who had come on board shortly before the hour of sailing, and had proved a most exacting and (from the point of view of a cabin steward) unsatisfactory passenger. He had required constant attendance, as those who are little used to command the services of others are often disposed to do when the opportunity becomes theirs, and he had left the boat without bestowing the gratuity which all stewards expect to get. It was clear that Fenner would be both able and willing to supply the absolute identification that the occasion required.

It was arranged that he should call at Scotland Yard next morning, when a written statement could be taken from him, and arrangements made for his attendance at the trial of the accused man. If the *Manhattan* should dock punctually at Southampton, it might be possible to bring Tony into the magistrate's court before the *American Merchant* would be due to leave, and Fenner might give his evidence, and still sail upon her, and be back in England again before the date of the trial in the superior court.

So it was arranged; and Inspector Combridge might have returned to Scotland Yard in as self-congratulatory a mood as that in which he had left it a few hours before, had he not encountered the chief engineer, a four-chevroned officer as important as the commander himself, and listened politely to an account of the punctuality and reliability of the ten-day boats of the *American Merchant* line, in contrast to alleged qualities of those of the faster Southampton services.

Inspector Combridge had neither knowledge to qualify him to dispute this prideful assertion nor disposition to do so, and the conversation would have ended with the minimum of assenting murmurs that an indifferent politeness required, had not the engineer worded his final asseveration in a way that invited qualification.

"Every Friday night for the last I don't remember how many years, one of these boats has left the dock here, and every Monday week following you could see her tying up at Boston or New York, as regular as though there wasn't a fog on the banks, or a storm anywhere from—"

"Every Saturday night, I expect you mean," Inspector Combridge interposed, with the sailing date of February 21st on his mind.

"No, it's Friday night we always leave here. If anyone gets Saturday into his head, he'll come to an empty quay."

"I don't know what your general practice may be," Inspector Combridge replied, with a stubborn refusal to recognize a possibility of which, with a stupefying confusion, he was already becoming subconsciously cognizant, "but I know you sailed on a Saturday night once at least, and only a few weeks ago."

"You can't know what isn't true. Someone's been pulling you leg if they told you that."

"I had it from your own office this afternoon. Saturday, February 21st."

"Well, so it might be if we were a bit after midnight in putting off. But you'd still call it Friday night. You wouldn't call it Saturday morning at 12:15."

"Perhaps I shouldn't, but I suppose I ought to. I expect you're right. I really don't know," Inspector Combridge answered, scarcely conscious of what he said. He had too much common sense and perhaps too little imagination—to doubt the fact. He had listened to a man who talked of that which he knew. But, all the same, it was an impossible thing.

So he protested next moment, his mind engaging, as it were, in a rearguard action of reluctant retreat. "But it isn't possible. There was a man on the boat who'd committed a murder in London that Saturday afternoon."

"Someone's kidded you into believing that? Well, I should call him a spry guy."

Inspector Combridge did not interest himself to learn whether the man so designated were the one who had sailed from London on Friday night or the one supposed to have "kidded" him to such a belief.

He said good night hurriedly, and disappeared down the gangway.

CHAPTER XXX.

A Quandary for the Yard

CHIEF INSPECTOR COMBRIDGE did not go back to Scotland Yard. It was already late, and he felt the need for thought, of which he had more than enough during the long hours of a sleepless night.

But his thoughts did not go far. They moved backward and forward in a narrow track, like a captured beast pacing a cage. He saw three possibilities, each of which his mind rejected in turn while allowing with cornered reluctance that one of them must be true. Either the last entry in Adrian Rissole's diary was forged, or the Chelsea-Brentford match had taken place on Friday, or Tony Rissole was innocent. That was the choice.

He felt certain that the diary had not been forged, and equally so that the match had been played on Saturday afternoon (that at least could be verified!), and consequently Tony was an innocent man.

He felt certain that Tony had committed the crime, and therefore, if the diary were not forged, the match *had* been played on Friday, or if the match had not been played on Friday, that last entry *had* been forged. There was no other possibility. The contingency of the activities of disembodied spirits is not regarded seriously by the C.I.D.

His mind vexing itself vainly among these scarcely credible choices, he told himself that he was foolish to worry further until he should have eliminated the one possibility which could be resolved with certainty. But this resolution would not bring the sleep he sought, and he was a wearied and worried man when he rang up the Football Association next morning to enquire the date of Chelsea's home fixture with the Brentford club.

Information is rarely refused when the enquiry is in the name of the C.I.D. The reply was almost instantly given. "February 21st."

"That would be a Saturday?"

"Yes. Of course. Saturday the 21st."

"It's quite certain it wasn't played a day earlier?"

There was a moment's delay while a calendar was consulted. "No, Saturday was the 21st."

"I mean that it couldn't have been played on the Friday?"

There was a note of amusement in the answering voice. "No, league matches aren't played on Friday."

"I thought that there are some exceptions to the Saturday rule."

"So there are. But they're always earlier in the week, except sometimes on Good Friday. I'll give you that. Anyhow, this one wasn't."

The answers had become somewhat impatient: the tone, if not words, said: "Even a policeman ought to know that." Inspector Combridge hung up the receiver, recognizing defeat.

The matter had become one that could no longer be kept to himself; which, indeed, he had no desire to do. And, besides, the next step must surely be to examine the diary, which was in Superintendent Davis's safe. He went into the superintendent's room.

Superintendent Davis looked up as he entered. "What's the matter, Combridge? I haven't seen you look worse since—"

"I haven't felt worse since I don't know when. What should you say if Tony Rissole turns out to be the wrong man?"

"I should say you're a bit late finding it out. I suppose you've got something fresh against Lovejoy?"

"No. It's worse than that. We've simply got to drop Tony out. All the trouble we've been to has just gone to prove that it wasn't him. "

"I suppose you don't mind telling me what this proof is?"

"Antonio Gardini was Tony Rissole. There's nothing surer than that. And Antonio sailed from London half an hour after midnight on Friday."

Superintendent Davis became silent, rubbing his chin. He took such jests of fortune more phlegmatically than Inspector Combridge was able to do, but he foresaw an unpleasant time. "I suppose it's quite certain that Tony didn't get someone to impersonate him?" he suggested, being perhaps the only utterance of complete folly which had ever passed his deliberate lips.

"I thought of that. But it doesn't make sense. He wouldn't get anyone to impersonate being someone else. And if he did—well, it's all too elaborate and he doesn't sound the kind of man who would think it out, or have the connections or resources for such a plot."

"Yes. It was an absurd suggestion, which I ought not to have made. But I had a feeling that there was something wrong about the sailing date of that boat. I was on the track of it when Mr. Jellipot mentioned the boat, and then something else put it out of my mind. As a matter of fact, I knew when those boats sail. But it would have been too late to do anything useful then."

"I don't know about that. It'd be something if we can put the right man into the dock when we have to let Tony go."

"So it would. But we haven't let him go yet. I wonder what Mr. Jellipot's going to say to this. I thought he was never wrong!"

"He'll say we ought to have told him about the diary before."

"So you should. I thought when the time came we agreed he was to be fully informed."

"Well, I didn't. I told him everything else. I didn't happen to mention that."

Superintendent Davis frowned, checking a sarcastic word. In an association of fifteen years, the two men had never been as near to an open quarrel as they were then. It was a position in which one, if not both, was likely to have to bear an official censure, if nothing worse, and it was hard not to throw responsibility on another's back.

There was some generosity as well as a shrewdness in the remark he substituted for that unspoken rebuke: "Well, that doesn't make much difference, as I see it. Jellipot would have been just as wrong if the diary hadn't existed at all. We said we'd follow his judgment, and it's for him to show us the way out of the mess that he's dropped us in."

"You want me to see Jellipot, show him the diary, and ask him what he can make of that?"

"No one could make anything of it but what it says. I want you to rub it in that he's made fools of us—or led us to make fools of ourselves—and use his wits—he's got more than most, I'll allow that—to show us the best way out. The real criminal would be better than nothing. You were right there. He might at least show us him."

"It must be Lovejoy, after all. That looks like a safe bet now."

"Or Vestman. Suppose all this passport business was just a blind to turn suspicion away from himself?"

"I don't see how it could have been that. But I don't know. I've thought till I can't think any more. I just feel muddled up."

"You need a stiff whisky-and-soda," Superintendent Davis, who had great faith in the effect of a moderate measure of alcohol, replied "You'd better go to Jellipot now, and give the headache to him. You can tell him that there's no time to lose. The *Manhattan*'s due to dock at two P.M. today."

Inspector Combridge stood in obvious hesitation. "I don't want to make us look fools to him. I can't help thinking it's Tony, in spite of everything, and if so, there must be some explanation, and I don't want to hear it from him.

"Suppose that last page was forged?"

"Suppose it wasn't." The sarcasm of irritation had returned to Superintendent Davis's voice as he said this. But he got up, and fetched the diary from the safe. The two men bent over it together.

Certainly, if that last entry were a forgery, it was one of the cleverest they had ever seen. And was it possible that Tony Rissole should have had such skill, even had he the brains to think of the device, or the time to execute that which could not be done in a casual manner?

"Poynter might have managed it," Superintendent Davis said thoughtfully, his mind searching every possibility, however remote.

"Well, we'll see what Mr. Jellipot says," Inspector Combridge replied. He felt that there would be some satisfaction in demonstrating to the solicitor that he had fallen into the same error as they, and a frailer hope that he could propose something which would justify the extradition. "But," he added, "I shall have to take him the book. He's sure to want to see that for himself."

But as he said this, a thought came to him. He looked up from the book which was now in his hand, to meet the superintendent's eyes, and to know that the temptation had come to both. No one knew of the diary except themselves. Its existence was no more than a fortuitous fact. The case against Tony Rissole was, and could be, no more than it would have been if Adrian had not kept a diary at all, which it was in no way incumbent upon him to do. Only they knew that it existed, and only by its production could they bring confusion to the evidence against Tony Rissole which they had been at so much trouble to obtain. *And that evidence was entirely true.* That of the diary did not shake it at all. It only made nonsense of the conclusion which might be reasonably deduced therefrom. There would be a strong *prima facie* case to justify the extradition, but it need not be pressed too hard. The elements of doubt might be admitted in court to a point which would ensure acquittal. No jury likes to bring in a verdict of guilty in such a case if they can see a doubt, be it as small as it may. In imagination, with which he was well endowed, Superintendent Davis may have heard the judge complimenting the prosecution for the scrupulous fairness with which it had been conducted. "You'd better let Mr. Jellipot see it," he said, "but, of course, you mustn't leave it with him. It mustn't pass out of our hands."

"Oh, he won't expect that. I only wonder who he'll tell us to arrest now."

"It shows," Superintendent Davis reflected, when he was left alone, "that you never know how a case will end. Not till you see the judge putting on the black cap. I suppose we shall be running in Lovejoy now."

With this thought he put the case resolutely out of his mind. It would be waste of time to consider it further until Combridge should return, and meanwhile he had much else to do, but all the same he would have liked to see Jellipot's face when…. He chuckled to himself at the thought.

CHAPTER XXXI.

MR. JELLIPOT DOES A GOOD DEED

UNLIKE Inspector Combridge, Mr. Jellipot had slept well. He had dismissed from his mind any doubt of the guilt of Tony Rissole, or the innocence of Edwin Lovejoy, and his thoughts during the previous day had been largely occupied by his promise to the ironmonger's wife, which it had become time to redeem.

He had not forgotten the assurance he had given her, that her levity of conduct should not first come to her husband's knowledge through evidence in a public court, and he knew that Tony was about to be landed at Southampton, and must be brought before a magistrate immediately.

It was true that this would, almost certainly, be no more than a formal remand on the first occasion, and that, even at a later hearing, it was probable that whatever legal gentlemen might be acting for the accused carpenter would consent to a committal, without disclosing their line of defence; but the risk of some damaging reference to Jane Lovejoy being made, however small, was one which he felt that he had no right to take.

So, while Inspector Combridge had been on the way to his disconcerting visit to the *American Merchant*, Mr. Jellipot had been dictating a letter to Edwin Lovejoy, asking him to give him a call. He said nothing of the nature of the business on which he wished to see him, feeling come confidence that he would come without that, and not wishing to disturb his mind in advance. Superintendent Davis would have had an added sense of the irony of the situation, and perhaps an increased amusement at the dilemma which Mr. Jellipot must be preparing for himself, could he have heard the conversation which was proceeding in the solicitor's office, even while Inspector Combridge revealed the bomb which was so near to exploding beneath their feet.

"You look," Mr. Jellipot said, as Edwin Lovejoy seated himself in the usual chair at his left hand, "in better health than when you were last here."

"I'm a good bit less worried than I was then, thanks—well, thanks a good deal to you."

"I am not aware that I have done much to deserve thanks. In fact, I have felt that I owe you some apology for having—perhaps unavoidably—been the one who first acquainted you with a suspicion—an entirely unfounded suspicion, as we know now—under which you lay, and which you were naturally disposed to resent.

"It is that matter, and another arising therefrom, on which I have asked you to see me now. And if we should dispose of that in the way I hope it may be possible to do, there may be a third which also should be of some interest to you."

Mr. Lovejoy heard this with no apprehension of any evil to come. He looked a different man from the harassed debtor who had sat in that chair a few weeks before. He had put on weight. He was more carefully dressed. He looked as though his digestion were more at ease. And there was a kindliness in Mr. Jellipot's manner, a soothing quality in his leisurely periods, which were unsuggestive of any further trouble to come.

"In the first place," Mr. Jellipot went on, "I am pleased to be able to tell you that you can, so far as I am able to judge, put any further apprehension concerning a charge being made against yourself absolutely aside. More than that—and, unless you have come in contact with such an experience, you may hardly realize how much it is—you will be relieved of the shadow of having been associated with an unsolved crime. Tony Rissole, as you may know from the public press, is being landed in England today. Until he is convicted, he may be technically an innocent man, and we must not prejudge his guilt; but speaking in the privacy of this office, and to one as much concerned as yourself, I will say that the evidence against him—of much of which you are unaware—is of so convincing a character that I think there is little doubt that that conviction will be obtained."

"Well, I can't say I shan't be glad about that. I don't like to think of any man being hanged, but one who'd stab another like that when he wasn't looking—it isn't easy to have mercy on him."

"It is an opinion with which I am disposed to agree. We may dismiss Tony Rissole from our minds, except so far as he comes into the second matter which it has become my duty—my rather difficult duty—to discuss with you. You will pardon me if I ask a question which may seem impertinent, which it is not meant to be. But are your recent relations with Mrs. Lovejoy all that, as a companion and husband, you can desire?"

The question was evidently unexpected. Mr. Lovejoy flushed angrily. But Mr. Jellipot noticed that the suggestion was not denied. "Do you mean that she's told you that?"

"Yes. And I may add that it was causing her much distress." The ironmonger looked as though he hardly knew how to take this, but was not displeased. "Then I don't see," he answered, "why she keeps it up as she does."

"Well, perhaps even that may become clear. But I was first concerned to establish that there is something which, for your common happiness, should be cleared away. Have you had any idea of the cause of the measure of estrangement of which you are both aware?"

"I thought," Mr. Lovejoy replied, with a bitter bluntness, "that she wasn't quite sure that I hadn't done Adrian in myself."

"Then you can put that aside. If she ever had such a doubt, she may have been disposed to blame herself rather than you, and it is one which, I am quite sure, she no longer holds. Apart from that, have you no idea of what may be on her mind?"

"I've thought that she got different after she knew that she'd got money."

"Then I am happy to say that you can put that idea absolutely aside also. I do not say that the fact of her financial independence is entirely irrelevant. If under any circumstances you should separate...."

"You mean she asked you to propose that?" There was an astonished anger in Mr. Lovejoy's voice as he interrupted with this exclamation. It was evidently a word he had not expected to hear.

"No. I am sure she has no such wish, and, if she had, it would, on my present information, have no support from me. The position is precisely opposite. She is apprehensive that the proposal may come from you."

"Then she's a little fool, as she always was. I've never been anything but a good husband to her."

"It is much," Mr. Jellipot conceded, with a dryness of tone of which his auditor was not unaware, "to be sure of that. But you have allowed that your recent relations have not been all that either of you could desire."

"They've been a bit better the last few days."

"That, I suggest, is because she has felt some relief in the knowledge that she had confided in me. But I must still ask you, have you no other idea as to what may be causing this unhappiness, which appears to have become more acute, if it has not entirely originated, since Adrian Rissole's death?"

There was a perceptible pause following this question, and Mr. Jellipot was expecting a negative or evasive answer; but when it came, in a tone of angry irritation, it was of a blunt directness: "I suppose you've got to have it. I think she'd been carrying on with Adrian more than she should, and she can't get it off her mind now. She may have wondered whether I killed him because of that. And the idea never crossed my mind till she let it out by fibbing when there wasn't any need if she'd got nothing to hide."

"Then you were exactly right, and there is little more for me to say, except this, that she will have no peace till she knows that you are aware of all that occurred, and that you both agree to forget.

"But I ought to add," Mr. Jellipot continued in his most deliberate manner, "that her misconduct was not with Adrian Rissole alone. She knew Tony also, and they appear to have quarrelled on her account—in particular, because Tony apprehended that Adrian's money would be left to her."

The ironmonger heard this with angry eyes and a hard-set mouth. Mr. Jellipot, regarding him gravely, could observe no mercy in what he saw. But when he did speak at last, the words might have been worse. "I'd like to thrash her till she can't stand."

"It would be a course of action," Mr. Jellipot replied, "which the law does not approve, but for which I should not blame you at all. But you might consider whether kindness might not be a better course."

"Or just tell her to clear out."

"Yes. You could do that. But there are factors in the problem which you should not entirely fail to observe. There is a proverb that Nature abhors a vacuum, which may not be entirely beside the mark."

"You mean," Mr. Lovejoy retorted with instant perception of the implication of this remark, "that I left Jane too much alone?"

"Scarcely that. I do not see how that could have been avoided, or that a woman should be considered unfit to trust during such necessary separations. It was when you were together that you may have left her too much alone."

"Well, that's plain. You've heard her side, but not mine, which you never will. I've got to do some talking to her." Mr. Lovejoy rose, as though there were no more to be said, and Mr. Jellipot, being still in some doubt, though not much, as to what the outcome of this matrimonial difference would be, might have let him go with no further words, but he stopped abruptly, and sat down again, as a new thought entered his mind. "I suppose all this will come out when Tony Rissole's tried?"

"It is possible that it will."

"They'll want Jane in the box?"

"She must be prepared to be called."

"Then she'll get what she deserves."

"She must be prepared for a very worrying time. It will be one when she may be particularly responsive to comfort, sympathy, and advice from you."

"Well, that's one way of looking at it."

"It would be, I think, an opportunity which you should not miss."

Mr. Lovejoy got up again. "If," he said, "she can talk half as well for herself as you can for her—"

"It is not a reasonable supposition. She will be emotionally disturbed. It is a position in which you should, I suggest, go halfway, or, perhaps, somewhat further than that."

"You wouldn't say I should give her a present for being good?"

"Not, perhaps, for that. But the idea is, in itself, excellent."

Mr. Lovejoy appeared to be reduced to silence by that reply. He had shaken hands already, and now made for the door. Mr. Jellipot was hesitant as to calling him back for that which might, or might not, be better proposed on a later day, when he burst out again: "It's no good. You've put it all very cleverly. You've almost made me feel I ought to apologize to her for what she's done. But she'll have to clear out, all the same. I'm not going to live on that money."

"That," Mr. Jellipot replied, leaving his visitor to come back at his own pace to the waiting chair, "is very much how I expected that you would feel, but it is a position that need not arise. Do you mind telling me at what price you value your business in Hornsey Road?"

"I'm not going to sell it to her, if you mean that."

"On the contrary, I should advise her strongly against buying it, if she were anxious to do so. I have been seriously apprehensive lest her money should be lost in that direction."

"Then you can put it out of your mind. There'll be not a penny more I shall take, and I'll find some way to pay back—"

"That is what I wish to help you to do. Do you mind telling me what I asked?"

"I gave £1,000 for the goodwill alone. I'd been eight years saving that, and three years more to get what I spent on the first stock."

"Do you honestly think it is worth more than that now?"

"You know it isn't. The goodwill's worth next to nothing at all."

"Then will you—yes, sit down by all means, and listen carefully to what I am going to say.

"You have had a hard fight, and have been most conscious of your own troubles, and loss of profits. How do you suppose your opponents have felt about it?"

"I hope I've made them feel a bit sick once or twice. Especially when I've stocked one of their leading lines and sold out at cost, just to give them a nasty jolt."

"You have made them feel very sick indeed. When I informed them that substantial additional capital might be available to enable you to continue the struggle—"

"You mean you've been in communication with them?"

"I took that liberty. Not, of course, as acting for you, which I was not. I have obtained a written offer from them to pay £3,000 for the goodwill and possession. The stock would be taken at a valuation."

"I'm not going to sell out to them. "

"Then you will be excessively foolish. You can withdraw now with a large profit, and—shall I say, with the honours of war? You can continue the fight, and give them the satisfaction of ruining you, and gain nothing better than your own bankruptcy. I had thought that you were a wiser man."

Mr. Lovejoy sat in gloomy silence while his mind adjusted itself to a new fact, and a new view. Then he said: "You'd better give me a pen."

"You mean you will give me written instructions to accept the offer?"

"Yes. I don't care how soon it's done."

"It is a wise decision. You will have the means of acquiring a better business, in a position where, we may hope, no similar trouble will occur. And for Mrs. Lovejoy it will mean new surroundings, where old memories will more quietly die."

"It will be out of England for me."

"That also may be a wise decision. I sometimes think, if I were a younger man—"

"I should say you're doing well enough here. I'd never guessed a lawyer could be a good man."

With this left-handed compliment to an honourable profession, Edwin Lovejoy finally left the room.

CHAPTER XXXII.

IT WAS AS SIMPLE AS THAT

MR. Lovejoy went out, and Inspector Combridge, almost immediately afterwards, entered Mr. Jellipot's room. The two men had passed each other in the passage, when Mr. Lovejoy had been surprisingly affable to a man whom he had found no reason to like, and the inspector had been even colder than usual in his response.

"I see you've just had Lovejoy here," he said gloomily, as he sat down. "It's about that beastly case I've got to see you again."

"You mean the Rissole case isn't going well?"

"No. It's gone straight on to the rocks. We've come on the worst snag we've had yet."

"Then," Mr. Jellipot replied, unperturbed by this outburst, "you'll be additionally glad to know that I have been able to render you a small service in that connection. I think you can anticipate with confidence that Mrs. Lovejoy will prove to be a reliable and most important witness. She will be prepared to tell the truth with as little reserve as most women, placed in her uncomfortable position would be likely to do."

"I don't know that that's saying much."

"I am not sure that it is. She may possibly do somewhat better, than that."

"The first question is whether there'll be a trial at all, and who'll be in the dock if there is. What'll she be likely to say if her husband's there?"

Mr. Jellipot looked serious. "It is a proposition," he said, "which I see no occasion to entertain."

"No? Well, it wasn't Tony. We know that."

"Then there is little more to be said. But I am surprised. The evidence against him is very strong."

"But unfortunately we've been going to a lot of trouble to prove that it's much stronger the other way. Tony sailed on the *American Merchant*, you'll agree there?"

"I have no reason to doubt it. If he can be identified with—"

"Well, he can. His cabin steward recognized his photo at once. There's no doubt it was him, and that's where we're in it up to the neck. The boat didn't really sail on Saturday. It left at 12:30 on Friday night."

"So I have already understood. But there is surely no difficulty there. It was on Friday night that Mr. Lovejoy saw him slinking down the stairs, no doubt just after the murder had been done."

"Oh, what Lovejoy saw! I wish I felt that we could get the truth out of him. But it's no use beating round the bush. We know that Adrian was alive on the next day. He went to a football match on Saturday afternoon."

"It would require very strong evidence to convince me of that. May I ask why you are so sure on that point?"

"Because—well, Superintendent Davis agreed that I ought to show you this."

With a rather shamefaced expression, Inspector Combridge handed over the book which he had not mentioned before.

Mr. Jellipot took it in silence. He turned the leaves until he came to that final entry, which he read with care, but with no indication of what he thought. He handed it back with the remark: "Poor fellow. I believe football was the greatest interest that he had."

"And that's all you make of that?"

"No. I regard it as evidence of the utmost value. It is conclusive, to my mind, as to the date on which the murder occurred."

"That's the trouble we've got to face."

"I am not sure that trouble is the right word. Am I right in supposing that you have had this book from the day that you searched the flat?"

Inspector Combridge looked uncomfortable again, but it was not a position in which anything less than the full truth would avail.

"Yes. Superintendent Davis didn't wish me to mention it at first. He thought the fewer who knew the more likely it was that the murderer would put his foot in it by making up the wrong tale. If you think it's a fake, I should say you're wrong."

"I had no such thought. I recognized Adrian Rissole's writing without difficulty, and it is a book of the existence of which I already knew. As to concealing it from me, you were within your right, but, if you will pardon me saying so, you were unwise. You would have saved yourself some anxious moments had you told me earlier."

"Perhaps I should. But the question is what are we to do now?"

"You will include the book in the exhibits to which you will invite the attention of the defence, and you will call me to give evidence upon it."

"You mean we are to go on with the prosecution of Tony Rissole?"

"Yes. I believe him to be a guilty man. I suppose you have read that diary, which I have had no opportunity of doing? Then may I ask whether there are any entries of importance relating to Mrs. Lovejoy?"

"Yes. One or two. But what—"

"Because as her solicitor I shall be glad to have an opportunity of considering them. Not now. At another time. There is also I suppose—I may say I know—an entry of the date on which Adrian called here to instruct me concerning his final will?"

"Yes. We noticed that. I wonder how you—"

"Very simply, Adrian told me about it. Incidentally, I recall that I was on the point of telling you this on one occasion when other matters, doubtless of more immediate importance, were permitted to supervene. Adrian was a man of particularly procrastinating disposition, of which he was aware, and which he used various devices to overcome.

"When he saw me, he happened to mention that he had entered the call in his diary on the previous evening, in advance of the event, but for which he would probably have let the day go by without bringing his purpose to the point of action. He said that he frequently adopted this device, which he called burning his boats, an expedient which is not an exact analogy; but was, I believe, actually adopted by Hernando Cortez, and other—"

"You mean he wrote it the night before to keep himself up to scratch?"

"Yes. I mean he wrote it the night before. That is what I was attempting to say."

"Well, that lets us out, if you'll get any jury to believe it. It takes swallowing, especially if he was fond of football. You wouldn't tell me that he'd want to go to a match, and couldn't bring himself to put on his boots unless he'd written down that he'd done it the night before?"

"No. That would be absurd. It was matters for which he had no appetite, and which could be put off from day today, to which that method would be applied. I suggest that it was P's account—

whoever P may be—that he was resolved to bring himself to the point of settling before he went to the match, which is the reason why that entry was made.

"You will remember that Adrian was slightly lame. Walking may have been no pleasure to him. The payment of the account may have involved an effort he was disinclined to make—this is, of course, no more than a probable guess. But he may have gone out on that Friday afternoon resolved to make this call, and returned after irresolutely substituting a shorter walk. Reproaching himself for this, he resolves that there shall be no similar procrastination on the next day. And so, as he enters his flat for the last time, he makes this entry in his diary to ensure that his next day's resolution will he sufficient to take him to his creditor's door before he goes to his own enjoyment. It was, of course, the whim—the foolish, illogical whim—of a lonely man, but it is very far from being an incredible thing."

"And I've always said that what can't speak can't lie!"

"You wish me to believe that you have taken that proverb seriously?"

Mr. Jellipot looked surprised.

www.ingramcontent.com/pod-product-compliance
Lightning Source LLC
Chambersburg PA
CBHW020646180626
46816CB00003B/1140